CW01424846

PENNY

YES MORE

LOVE

Paul

X

To Mum, Dad and Stephen

The Idea

'What do you mean, you split up playing crazy golf? Who splits up playing crazy golf, Danny?!'

'She kicked the ball through the windmill.'

'She kicked the ball through the wi….so what!? It was only your third date with her and you'd already said 'she might be the one'. The art museum…the bike ride…remember? You liked her.'

'I'm too competitive. You can't kick the ball through the windmill. And she'd already taken six shots.'

'You're an idiot. You split up because of THAT?'

'Well, there was more to it than that. There just wasn't the right… chemistry? We were like mute dolphins.'

'Mute dolphins?'

'We just didn't click.'

'You're an idiot.'

He was right. Tom's always right. I am an idiot. But every idiot has at least one good idea.

A drawer full of diaries with page after page containing details of failed relationships. I'm 38 years old. I've got a chequered dating history. I've been in love a couple of times…but still haven't found the one.

But the more dates you have the better you get at it, right?

Experience is everything in these situations. And chemistry. Chemistry is important. But what else?

Ideas.

Ideas are important. And I've finally had mine.

'How many dates does it take to find 'The One'?'

This particular idiot believes its twenty-six. Twenty-six dates are enough to get to know someone well enough to decide if you want to maybe spend the rest of your lives together.

And as coincidence would have it, there are twenty-six letters in the alphabet. So, I'm going to try and reach the letter Z…twenty-six dates with one person…and then who knows?

Maybe pop the question?

Which leads us to another question. Is Rocky Balboa the only person to have ever proposed in a zoo before?

Tom brought two drinks back to the table. And salted peanuts. Always with the salted peanuts. We'd already been discussing our latest light hearted money-making idea. A gymnasium for religious people called Jehovah's Fitness.

'Jesus Christ, Tom, how big are your hands? How can you carry two pints with one hand?'

'Look, just because you've got dainty office worker hands, don't be having a go at mine. I've got a proper outdoors job.'

'But your fingers. Look at them. It's like someone's chopped your original ones off and sellotaped five Biscuit Boosts to a fist.'

'Look, never mind my chocolate fingers, Danny. How did the ice skating with Gemma go? The letter 'I'…what's that, the ninth letter? The ninth date?'

'The ice skating was fine.Yeah, date number nine and I stayed upright. Plus, we were holding hands a lot. I'm GREAT at holdings hands.'

'That sounds promising ...so then what?'

'We went back to her flat...had a couple of drinks...went upstairs and that's when it happened.'

'*IT* happened?! You mean you had sex? We're 38 years old, not teenagers, come on, what happened? Spill.'

'She asked me to talk dirty.'

'Oh...'

'I can't talk dirty, Tom. I act stupid. She said I'd been a naughty boy and asked me what I'd done.'

'There's not going to be a tenth date is there?'

'I don't think so.'

'So, you'd been a naughty boy? What did you tell her you'd done?'

'Well, I leant into her ear and I whispered softly. Dominantly...but softly.'

'Yeah ok, Christian Grey. What did you say?'

'I said yeah, I've been naughty...I've spilt red wine all over the living room carpet.'

'You're an idiot.'

It was my turn to bring two drinks back to the table. And more salted peanuts of course. I placed them down onto the table with my normal size hands and Tom was already looking deep in thought.

'I saw something on Tik Tok the other day, Danny, and it made me think of you.'

'Tik Tok?? What are you, 14 years old?'

'There's good stuff on Tik Tok!'

'No there isn't. You probably waste two hours a day watching dogs pretend to DJ or watching loveless couples in dead end relationships pretending to prank each other in an attempt to rekindle something in their relationship that they probably never even had.'

'Well, yes…there's that. But there's other stuff too.'

'Ok like what?'

'So, there's this guy. He says he knows how you can find the person you want…and the person you need to be…for that person to find you.'

'No DJ-ing dogs?'

'No DJ-ing dogs.'

'No loveless prank couples?'

'No loveless prank couples.'

'Ok, continue.'

'You need to be free.'

'I am free. Me and Gemma are finished.'

'You need to be happy to attract a kind person.'

'I'm happy. You're here. We've got a beer each. We've got peanuts.'

'You need to have life skills.'

'I have life skills. I open boxes of eggs and check them before I buy them.'

'You need to be caring. You need to be healthy, vibrant and alive.'

'You know me more than anyone else, Tom. I'm those things. And I'm alive. I'm sat opposite you now, look. Hi.'

'Yes, hi. He says you need to have a good appearance.'

'I've got a good appearance!'

5

'You've got a salted peanut in your beard.'

'So, what else, Tom?'

'So, you think about this person on a regular basis and then BOOM! That person will walk into your life. The universe will send them to you.'

I stared at Tom. Picked the salted peanut from my beard. Contemplated what he'd just told me, before looking at him straight in the eye.

'It all sounds a little bit like Hocus Pocus.'

'You see, Danny, this is your problem. You need to open your mind a bit. You need to find Mrs Right. You're just interested in Mrs Right Now. Stop living your life like a game. Just be yourself. The right person will find you. And you'll find them.'

Ever since I'd met Tom as a shy sixteen-year-old, he'd taken me under his wing. Introducing me to new music, to a new way of thinking, to his Mum's Sunday roasts which would require a knife, a fork and also a stepladder in order to reach the mound of roast potatoes she'd piled on my plate. And he was still here…giving advice…being supportive…being open minded.

'Well maybe it's about to happen. I'm meeting Ellie on Friday night.'

So, this Alpha Male idea? Experiment? Game? It might sound a bit misleading.

But it's not what you think.

I'm not what you think.

Let me tell you a secret.

I'm not an Alpha Male.

There, I said it.

I can't be.

My gym playlist includes Like a Prayer by Madonna. I'm not dominant in social and professional situations. But I can hold my own. Not like that. Ok, sometimes like that. I'm single remember. Anyway, mind out of the gutter for a second, please. What I'm saying is that I don't feel I have to compete with others to be the best. Or to eat a gazelle. Or whatever it is Alpha Males endeavour to do. There's no point. Just be confident in yourself and be honest with people. Be consistent with people, walk confidently into rooms and don't slouch. And open doors for people. Always open doors for people.

'So, tell me one more time, what are the actual rules with this Alpha Male thing, then?'

'Tom… I'm glad you asked. Again. There is only one rule. I get to choose the letter 'A' date. And then she gets to choose the letter B date. And then vice versa until it all goes pear shaped. And if it does get to the letter Z, it falls on her choice. So, no pressure there.'

It's a very straight forward concept really. Unlike life.

Unlike love. Relationships can be difficult.

Let's go back to the beginning

Stacey Pointon

I was 16 when I lost my virginity. Stacey Pointon's Mum's living room. MTV hits of the 80s is playing in the background and she's on top of me, half-dressed and managing to look a lot sexier than I am. I've got a look of unbridled joy, blotchy excitement and pure shock on my face, as I momentarily look over Stacey's pale shoulder and see A-Ha's Morten Harket pulling his equally stunning blonde, permed girlfriend into a comic book.

Me and Stacey had met in a hardware store as weekend workers…We got on well and it was all a bit flirty. She told me she'd seen me stacking tins of Dulux in the stockroom and thought I was 'fit'. She also liked that I told the same joke to the old women who came into the shop looking for one particular item.

'Excuse me, son…have you got any turps?'

'Yeah sure. Do you want video turps or cassette turps?'

It doesn't sound very sexy, I know. This was more '50 Shades of Grey Paint.'

The sex was great. I mean, I didn't have any frame of reference at this point apart from watching a very old and worn copy of Michael Douglas and Sharon Stone going at it in Basic Instinct. And yes, I was nervous about the sex but I hadn't seen or felt anything as exciting and earth shatteringly enjoyable as this before in my life, probably since the first time I saw…well…Michael Douglas and Sharon Stone going at it in Basic Instinct.

As a clammy, flush faced and breathless Stacey Pointon dismounted, I looked down at my lap and got a bit of a shock. It looked…different. Bigger. Definitely redder. And had some 'bits' on it. Like crumbs maybe? Ok, it looked like a cross between Sir Alex Ferguson's face and a rhubarb crumble. Have I got a second dick? What's that? It looks like the bit in Alien where it opens his mouth and another mouth comes out. And to make things worse, my pubes actually look like Sigourney Weaver's hair in the same film.

I'm sporting a Ripley's Thatch as Stacey Pointon reaches over for the remote control to change channels. I should have shaved them a bit looking back but what do you know about manscaping at 16 years of age? I suppose I'd rather it looked like Ripley in Alien as opposed to Brian Glover in Alien 3 though. That's not a good look.

So how was it? My first time? At one point I think Stacey Pointon might have been thinking about Morten Harket as she took me on. Why wouldn't she? He's fucking beautiful. I might have been thinking about him myself at one point. But I was now a man. And I wanted to tell the world. But I was sat in someone else's living room, with a Charles and Diana tea towel on my lap covering what appeared to be a fluorescent, crumbly glowstick. But I had a smile the size and length of The Nostromo engulfing my fresh, teen face. I felt a mixture of pain, anxiety and incandescent joy. I wanted to shout from the rooftops.

But in Stace's, no one could hear me scream.

Amalia Restaurant

'Are you sure a restaurant is a good idea for a first date?' Tom was already raising his eyebrow at this decision.

'It's a nice restaurant! Italian. Classy. I want to make a good first impression. I think I like Ellie. From the pictures at least…and the texts…see seems…interesting. And interested.'

'But…what about the mess? You can be a messy eater, Danny. Salted peanuts, remember? I've never seen you eat a full packet without dropping at least four. What if you get meatballs? It'll be carnage. You'll look like Sonny from The Godfather.'

'I can EAT meatballs, Tom. Trust me. First date. I'm paying. Hey listen to this…I'm going to make her an offer she can't refuse.'

'Your Marlon Brando is TERRIBLE. Stop doing that with your hand as well. You look like a Mafia Jeremy Beadle. And the voice is rubbish. He's meant to be from Sicily, not Lagos.'

'Ok, no more accents. Not even my Donald Duck sneezing impression. I promise.'

It's a great impression. It's up there with my impression of Ronan Keating singing but it's a well-known fact that EVERYONE can do an impression of Ronan Keating singing. I was instantly attracted to Ellie the moment she breezed into Amalia.

Summery dress. Doc Martens.

Confidence exuding from her…but in a shy way. The caterpillars in my stomach had decided now was the time for metamorphosis into fully fledged butterflies as she approached the bar with her arms out. That's a good sign. I'm no body language expert but arms out for an embrace is good.

I noticed a woman behind Ellie smiling as we, in my mind, awkwardly hugged and pulled a *'Well, here we are!'* face to each other.

'Danny!'

'Hi Ellie.'

'I knew it!'

'Knew what?'

'Sagittarius! I knew as soon as I walked in. I can tell these things.'

Oh God. More hocus pocus.

'So, you like Italian food then, Ellie?' I was using all my best lines as we sat down.

'Who doesn't love Italian food!?' She loves food. Box ticked.

'You know who I don't like though, Danny?'

'Who?'

'These Italian celebrity chefs who pretend to get their words mixed up and say 'boobs' instead of 'omelette', despite being born and raised in Hertfordshire. Or the ones who force Hollyoaks actors to sit and eat sea bass at 10am while they ask them questions, which they don't even listen to the answer to. No one wants to see someone from Hollyoaks struggling to eat seabass at 10am. It's all rubbish don't you think?'

I started laughing. I'm in trouble now. She likes Italian food and she's made me laugh. I know we're only on the letter 'A' but this has started too well if anything, apart from the star sign mumbo jumbo.

'So, this erm…star sign thing, Ellie. Can you really tell if you like someone just from what part of the year they were born? Am I really a typical Sagittarius? Can you tell that already?'

'It's all in the stars, Danny! But no one listens to it. I'm telling you. There's a truth to it.'

'So, what's a typical Sagittarius? Sagittarian? Is that right? Sagittarian? What am I like?'

'Well…you have a magnetic quality which makes you attractive and very easy to like.'

'You got me. I'm a believer already.'

'No! There's more to it. You like to perform the complex dance of flirtation with potential partners.'

'I'm thinking about getting the meatballs. How's that for a flirty dance? Ordering balls of meat.'

Ellie laughed and pretended to fan her brow and exhaled heavily.

'Be still my beating heart! And also, Sagittarius, you're a generous lover who enjoys sex and connection.'

'Shall we have our meal first?'

Ellie laughed again. It was going well…so I continued the questioning.

'So, what about compatibility then? How would you know if I got on with an…Aries? You said you were an Aries, right?'

'Oh, we'd get on, Danny. I check these things. It was one of the first things I did. So, Aries and Sagittarius make great friends as well as lovers. We understand each other's optimistic views on life. I can

be a bit more sensitive than you and you're more likely to put your foot in your mouth and say something stupid...'

Danny...don't say *'Like I love you?'* Try saying the second thing that comes into your head for a change. Don't put your stupid fucking Sagittarian foot in your mouth already. Just order something off the menu like a normal human being would do.

'Bold choice, Danny. I'm impressed. Meatballs on a first date. I kind of like that.You know what, I think I'll get the same.'

Two hours, which flew by; and three glasses of red wine later, we stood up. I reached out and took Ellie by the hand and led us towards the door a bit more zig-zaggy and giggly than we had on our respective ways in but we were already planning a second date.

The lady sat at the bar was still there and tapped me on the shoulder as we walked past.

'Hey...the Sagittarius, right?'

'The...the what, sorry?'

'The Sagittarius. I was sat behind you when you and your girlfriend walked in'

Ellie had continued walking towards the exit, not knowing I'd been stopped in my tracks.

'Oh, she's not my girlfri...'

'Look, I'm sorry to stop you but it's just...every time I looked over, you two were laughing and touching hands. It's great to see a couple doing that. People are too invested in their phones in restaurants now. I love seeing dates like that.'

'Thanks! That's really nice of you to say. Oh, and you know what?'

'What?'

'We didn't spill a single meatball between us.'

A confused look. Typical. Someone gives me a compliment and I start talking about meatballs.

I text Ellie two days later.

'Hi Ellie…you know what we spoke about…have you had a chance to think about anywhere beginning with letter B yet?'

'Hey Danny. Remember that bookstore I was telling you about? x'

Roxanne Cooper

So, my virginity had been well and truly lost and mine and Stacey Pointon's romance was also well and truly fleeting. Maybe a month after the whole sex in front of A-Ha experience, Stacey Pointon was more interested in hunting high and low for her next fix of passion and my first official break up was imminent. I brushed it off as any inexperienced teenager would and had only really been heartbroken once up to this point. Infant school nativity and an Oscar winning Joseph performance by yours truly. Roxanne Cooper was my Mary…and refused to hold my hand as we traipsed around Bethlehem looking for somewhere to stay. I was distraught, my performance dipped, I forgot my big 'Have you any room at the Inn?' line and was subsequently relegated to playing a lamb the following year.

Bookstore

'What's in the bag, Danny?'

'This, Thomas, my good friend, is a present for Ellie. I got it from that polite card shop where there's always a member of staff waiting at the door to say have a nice day to you. Very polite shop.'

'I'll ask again. What's in the bag, Danny?'

I opened the bag and pulled out a tiny book.

'Well, we're going to a bookstore on Saturday, right. So, I thought I'd get her a book. I'm romantic like that. Here we go. 'The Little Book of Astrology'. Now I reckon it probably delves into each of the astrological signs and shows you how to interpret the cosmos, not only day-to-day but far ahead into the future. I also reckon you can probably allow this book to shine a light on how the stars can reveal a deeper understanding of yourself and others.'

'You're reading that off the back of the book.'

'Yeah, well I don't know anything about it do I? How do I know if an Aquarius gets on with a Capricorn or why a Taurus would never love a Libra? Surely, just be a nice person and treat people well. Then you won't attract idiots? It doesn't matter when the sun rises or if you were born on the cusp of Gemini or Scorpio. They're probably not even together but you know what I mean.'

'And what are you again? Sagittarius?'

'Yeah. Fun loving and flirtatious. But with a quiet and intelligent side as well. I can also be…sagi-serious'

Tom raised the familiar eyebrow. The eyebrow I'd seen raised hundreds of times before. He hated that joke, I could tell.

'Please, please never ever say Sagi-serious ever again. She'll run a fucking mile.'

'Right, I'm off. Big date tomorrow. You can put your eyebrow down now'

We then attempted an awkward handshake / fist bump thing like most men in their late thirties, getting it completely wrong and therefore turning a simple goodbye into an emotionally underdeveloped impromptu game of Rock Paper Scissors.

'Danny!! Hey!! What's in the bag?'

'Hi Ellie. Just a little present. I got it from that polite card shop where there's always a member of staff waiting at the door to say have a nice day to you. Very polite shop.'

'Wooooo I LOVE presents. That's so thoughtful. I… I haven't brought you anything.'

Don't say *'You being here is enough'*. Don't say *'You being here is enough'* Don't say *'You being here is enough.'*

'That's ok. I wasn't expecting anything in return. I just thought you know. Bookstore. Book.'

Well done, Danny. You passed the test. Progress.

'Here you go…'

'The Little Book of Astrology!' I LOVE IT!!'

Ellie kissed me quickly on the cheek and turned to the back of the book.

'This book delves into each of the astrological signs and shows you how to interpret the cosmos, not only day-to-day but far ahead into

the future. Let this book shine a light on how the stars can reveal a deeper understanding of yourself and others. Danny, I love it! Hey, you should read it too.You never know, you might like it.'

'I mean I'll have a go. But...and please...I'm not being a dick, I swear...why do you think this kind of stuff helps you know if an Aries gets on with a Capricorn or why a Taurus will never love a Libra? Surely, just be a nice person and treat people well.Then you won't attract idiots?'

'I use it to sift out the idiots first. Simple as that. I'm a believer. Over the years I've discovered that you can work people out based on their signs.'

Ellie smiled a trusting smile at me. I looked at that little bit on the side of her mouth that I liked. A cross between a dimple and a crease. She's cute. And I never use the word cute.

'Come on Danny, let's go get a coffee and some cake.'

Cute, Coffee and Cake. If ever there was a sign a third date was imminent...this, was it.

'Your choice Danny! Where are we going for letter C?'

We'd had a lot of espresso but my heart pounded that little bit faster when she asked about a third date. I'd thought about it and maybe an opportunity to extinguish the previous crazy golf memory.

'Crazy golf? No chance, Danny. I'm too competitive for a start and you'll probably end up cheating, taking too many shots or kicking the ball through windmills. No chance.'

Had she been watching? Maybe she is magic after all.

Issie Green

I'm 18 years old and I'm sat in the Odeon with Issie Green. I don't want to look too pushy or desperate, so lead us not to the back row but to the penultimate row. A non-alpha move if ever there was one. We both have a tub of popcorn the size of our heads resting on our respective laps and it's awkward. It's a first date and we've made a terrible mistake. We're both quite shy and nervous and we're sat in a dark room, only turning to each other at the end of each trailer, to say *'That looks good.'* or *'That looks rubbish.'* It's hardly ideal. I'm wondering if she wants to be kissed. I'm wondering if I want to kiss her? Issie is a big fan of Ashton Kucher and we sit through the Butterfly Effect. A film based on the notion that the world is deeply interconnected, such that one small occurrence can influence a much larger complex system.

In other words, a small butterfly flapping its wings could hypothetically cause a typhoon.

Nonsense, I thought, as I got stuck into handful after handful of popcorn. Butterflies? What have butterflies got to do with anything.

Mine and Issie Green's linear paths were about to take a heavy diversion as she dumped me in a Yates wine lodge about a month later. Face to face. After being very articulately binned, I replied *'We could still go to the pictures again as mates if you want?'*

She looked at me and I knew what she was thinking. She was a lot more intelligent than me. Maybe she'll respond based on the Butterfly Effect? The choices we make today can shape our tomorrow?

'I don't think that would be a very good idea, Danny.'

Cinema

'*Before Sunrise? Never heard of it, Danny.*'

'*What? It's probably the most romantic film of all time. Well, one of them at least. Maybe this or True Romance. You know we were talking about chemistry and that we both have it? There's never been a chemistry like there is with these two. Not even with Clarence and Alabama. Ok, it helps if you look like Julie Delpy and Ethan Hawke, but...oh I can't wait for you to watch this. For us to watch this.*'

'*Can we get popcorn?*'

'*A tub as big as my head.*'

'*Ok I'll have to get more money out.*'

'*You're funny, Ellie.*'

And she was. It wasn't forced. Just a natural quick wit... coupled with that little dimple. The chemistry was something I couldn't put my finger on. But I could feel her eyes on me even when I looked away. And I couldn't take mine off her.

The film flew by.

'*That's us, Danny!! We're Julie Delpy and Ethan Hawke!!*'

'*No chance. Julie Delpy's got nothing on you. And Ethan Hawke's head is TINY*'

'*I LOVED IT. I LOVED IT!*'

'*You're spinning around. Be careful. You've had a lot of popcorn.*'

We went to get cake. Turns out we both love getting cake after a movie. I had a coffee. Ellie had a milky tea.

'Why don't you have some tea with your milk?'

'Shush Danny. You drink your drink. I'll drink mine.'

Ellie opened her phone and went straight to a movie quotes site.

'Come on Danny, lets re-enact that bit we spoke about.'

'What, here?'

'Yeah, come on, here, I'll send you the page as well. You're first.'

'But...'

'COME ON!! Aaaand ACTION!'

'Ok....er...Ellie, I feel like this is some kind of dream world we're in, y'know?'

'Yeah, it's so weird. It's like our time together is just ours. It's our own creation. It must be like I'm in your dream and you're in mine...or something?'

'And what's so cool is that this whole evening, all our time together, shouldn't be officially happening.'

'Yeah, I know. You wanted to play crazy golf.'

'Hang on, that wasn't in the film! Julie Delpy doesn't mention crazy golf once!'

Ellie laughed and smiled the smile.

'Only joking, Ethan...right I'll go to the bar. Alcohol this time? Two tequila sunrises?'

'Yeah. Two tequila sunrises. Nice.'

She walked past me but not before stopping to give me a

deep, full kiss on the lips. Jesus Christ, she can kiss.

Fuck.

'Two tequila sunrises. Here we go. And guess what? I've already thought about our letter D date. There's a couple of people I want you to meet.'

Gail Platt

I am still in my teens and I have had the misfortune of experiencing only my second wet dream. The person my subconscious has decided will star in this sticky wonderland is Gail Platt from Coronation Street. The previous wet dream wasn't long after playing the back end of a pantomime horse in a school play and having my face shoved right up close to Mandy Thomas' barely covered arse. Anyway, back to my Coronation Street moment and possibly my only saving grace was that I hadn't awoken in an Audrey Roberts induced gloopy mess. Liz McDonald, possibly the sexiest cast member at the time didn't get a look in, despite being an absolute shagger by all accounts.

Double Date

'You're going on a double date, Danny? Already?'

'Yeah. Is that too soon? Four dates in? Ellie's got a mate who's into horoscopes and tarot reading almost as much as she is, so...'

'And how are you getting on with that little book of astrology?'

'It's a slow burner. A page at a time maybe?'

'Well at least there's a complete stranger you can feel awkward with at this double date. You can speak to him rather than get involved in the space romance conversations.'

'His names Justin.'

'And what does Justin like?'

'I have no idea.'

'Well, you know the rules. If in doubt, ask him if he likes football and then just start shouting random 1990s footballers at each other for two hours. Easy.'

'I could do my Declan Rice joke.'

'What's your Declan Rice joke?'

'Declan Rice uses an inhaler? I didn't even know he was basmatic.'

Tom looked at me. He liked it. I knew he liked it. He didn't roll his eyes.

'Wendyyyyyyyyy!!!! It's so good to see you. Justinnnnnn!!!! How are you? This is... Dannyyyyyyyy.'

She'd never used that many 'y's in my name before.

What's happening?

'Hi Wendy… Hi Justin… nice to meet you both.'

We sat at the table…ordered food…and then the female members of our foursome pressed the astrology conversation button. And pressed it HARD.

'Ellie…you were right! Danny's a Sagittarius and you're an Aries…it was ALWAYS going to work. Hey, he's lovely. Lovely and tall.'

'I know, right…he's my lovely, tall Sagittarius. Hey, do you remember those last two?'

'The Pisces and the Scorpio?'

'The Pisces and the Scorpio.'

'Yeah, that was NEVER gonna work. Pair of them didn't stand a chance.'

'How's your sister, Wend? She still seeing that hypnotist?'

'Who, The Great Orgasmo? No, he was an oddball, him. Did you know he hypnotised one of her mates and told her to have an orgasm?'

'Whaaat?'

'Yeah, and it worked supposedly. Although when she came round, she had no idea she'd had one.'

'What?! How does that even work? He sounds more like a ro-hypnotist.'

'God knows. I asked her about it and she said she can't even remember tripping over and falling into the dog's water bowl.'

'Christ. Another bullet dodged there by the sounds of it, Wend. How's the foot anyway? At least the cast is off now, right?'

'God tell me about it. The itching was doing my head in. I'm blaming Mercury retrograde for it. Something always happens when it's Mercury retrograde doesn't it. Always has done with us two. What other time of the year would I have fallen down the stairs. Justin reckons I'm just clumsy but why would it happen now? Remember the last Mercury retrograde? That was when I almost sliced my finger off trying to julienne some carrots.'

'Yeah, I remember that.'

'Well anyway, I tried manifesting more positivity during the Lions Portal, so hopefully no more injuries. For a while at least.'

'Oh my god! Same here, it's the height of the Lions Portal this week you know? I told Danny that Sirius, Earth and Orion are all in alignment with each other, didn't I Danny? He's not listening. Told him on Tuesday I think.'

Me and Justin looked over at our dates as this conversation about busted ankles and injuries relating to julienned carrots somehow being caused by whichever way the sun was turning.

That's it. I'm making the first move. No more planet talk. No astrology from me. No more Mr Night Sky. I'm going in with both feet. I looked at Justin and spoke truly and from the heart.

'Morten Gamst Pedersen.'

'What?'

'Morten Gamst Pedersen.'

'What's that?'

'Oh. erm…do you support anyone, Justin? Football?'

'Football?? No chance mate. Bunch of wankers the lot of them. Give me a Grand Prix any day of the week. You've got to admire those

drivers. Proper sportsmen, don't you think?'

'I'm not really a fan of all that to be honest mate. I haven't even got an F1 button on my keyboard.'

Nothing. No reaction whatsoever. Tom loves that joke. Why isn't he laughing? Tom would be laughing. Ok maybe groaning…but reacting at least.

'You see, driving is the best thing in the world, Danny. Listen, I was travelling up to Stoke earlier in the week, Tuesday I think it was. No, Wednesday. I was going down the M6, really shifting, giving it beans, you know and the next minute the old sat-nav's telling me junction 17 at Sandbach is closed. Can you BELIEVE that? Closed!'

What is he talking about? These are just directions and destinations and detours. Fuck. Get him off the subject of junctions and QUICK. He'll be telling me about his favourite fucking service station next.

'Ah I'm not really into cars and driving to be honest Justin. I haven't even seen any of The Fast and The Furious films and I LOVE films. You…like films?'

'Kegworth Services.'

Fuck.

'Kegworth Services?'

'Best services in the UK mate. Ask me how much the petrol is. Go on, ask me.'

'How much is the petrol?'

'CHEAPEST IN THE UK MATE. Fill her up. Back on the M6. Edwyn Collins CD on full blast and BOOM! We. Are. Off.'

Edwyn Collins. I've got an Edwyn Collins joke. Try it.

Tom loves this joke.

'My er…my first ever girlfriend liked Edwyn Collins you know… AND she used to eat plants.'

'What? Why?'

'I don't know…but I'd never met a girl like herbivore.'

Nothing again?! My fucking god. Justin put his knife and fork down and headed to the toilets no doubt to throw up in disgust at my lame attempt to STOP HIM TALKING ABOUT FUCKING MOTORWAYS.

He walked back from the toilet, inexplicably started to do some shadow boxing and then sat down to begin his next attempt at trying to kill me with boredom. He didn't even come up for air as he rattled words at me like a machine gun, with no thought at all for punctuation.

'I always thought of getting a land rover you know just for that feeling of pure power it would be much better than the current car but I'm not resigned to having this one forever it's just hard sometimes with down payments and other things Wendy doesn't mind what I do but I'll just get it anyway you know when the times right I can see myself bombing down the A1 now I'd probably get it in black or maybe a dark blue.'

Jesus fucking Christ, man. At least put a full stop in somewhere or take a breath. I bet some people in prison haven't got sentences as long as that.

I just wanted to talk to Ellie but her and Wendy were still debating the benefits of solar eclipses.

'Dannyyyyy!'

'Hi, I'm still here.'

'You and Justin seem to be getting on well. Very chatty!'

'He's just been telling me about the best grab bag of Revels he's ever bought. Knutsford services, 2014. I almost tried to butt into the horoscope conversation.'

'Hey! There's no need for that. I'm gonna make you a believer, you'll see. Come on…let's make our excuses and leave, shall we?'

'You sure?

'Yeah, I'm tired…come on…I'll get you a grab bag of Revels on the way home. Which motorway do you think the taxi driver will take?'

The smile. The look into my eyes. I'm falling for her.

Holly Wilson

I'm now 19. A flitting relationship. Curly hair and a look of Jennifer Grey, better known for playing Baby in Dirty Dancing. I don't remember too much about the relationship apart from staying in her parents once, her getting up in the middle of the night, nudging me and saying 'I'm just going for a little tinkle' before making a noise which was less of a little tinkle and more of a 'hippopotamus trying to jet wash an Olympic size swimming pool'.

Hattie Freeman

Aged 20. First date. Kind of sat in silence…both awkward, until she blurted out *WHAT DID YOU HAVE FOR YOUR TEA, THEN?*' and the conversation somehow became even more stilted after that. I'd had fishcake, chips and beans, by the way.

I proceeded to order white wine from the very limited menu. A choice between either a half litre carafe or a litre carafe.

'We'll have a litre please.'

'Ooh Danny. Alita. You even know the name of the wines. Hey, they've spelt pasta wrong here.'

'That says pesto.'

I knew from this first date that me and Hattie Freeman wouldn't last long. I was still looking for my first love and it never even looked like being on the horizon.

Evening Stroll

'I love this idea, Danny! Don't you think it's easier to talk when you're out walking with someone? Rather than sat in the house? Just feels more natural, doesn't it?'

Ellie had turned up at my flat straight from work with a sports bag in tow.

'We're only going for a three mile walk Ellie, what's in the bag?'

'Have you ever tried walking three miles in heels?'

'Yes.'

'Knob. Gimme a second…quick change.'

'Hey. Come here.'

I pulled Ellie in close and moved her hair out of her eyes. My turn to instigate the long, deep kiss. I think it may have taken her aback slightly but she then pulled me in even closer.

She exhaled and stroked my cheek. And looked at me with her deep green manga comic eyes.

'Shall we stay in for a bit instead, Danny? We can still go walking…in a bit?

'I mean, the park will still be there later, I think?'

I pulled her in closer and whispered in her ear.

Then Ellie grabbed ME by MY hand and led me through MY bedroom door. I told you I wasn't an Alpha Male didn't I.

Ellie turned around. I pulled her in towards me, cupped her face and brushed her lips with mine, before kissing her more and more intensely.

And I closed my bedroom door.

That evening the park was full of families, couples, runners, single people all enjoying the outdoors.

This was my place of solace and had been for a while. Despite the crowds, I felt it was only me and Ellie there as we strolled…me grabbing her hand every so often. Her linking my arm every so often. Smiling at each other constantly.

'I'd always come and walk here while my dad wasn't well. And you're right you know, Ellie…it is a lot easier to talk when you're walking. Even if it's to yourself, asking 'What am I going to do? What can I do?'

'You haven't spoken much about your dad, Danny'

Ellie squoze my hand a little bit tighter and stroked my thumb with hers.

'Yeah, only if people bring him up really. I'll absolutely talk about everything he ever did for me, for the family…but sometimes I'm like, who wants to listen to that? But I'll talk about him to anyone. To you. Absolutely to you. Do you know what, I've never heard anyone eat an apple so noisily in my life. And so quickly. 3.2 seconds was his record, I think. The core, the pips, the lot. People were nice when he was ill. Some would say 'time heals everything'…but I don't really agree with that. It kind of means you're forgetting about that person or you're disregarding them. I don't think we ever fully get over people dying. You learn to cope with it and learn to live with it. But people shouldn't ignore the fact that a person is ill or has died. If people ignore it, it's like

saying that person's life doesn't or didn't count. And that's more hurtful. Spending all that time with my dad...someone who loved his family so much...I see it as a gift. And not everyone has been given that gift. So, I'm lucky, right?'

Ellie looked down at her trainers, which were now becoming covered with leaves.

'Yeah. You're right, Danny. It is a gift. And I'm here for you if you ever want to talk about it more.'

'I feel like talking now. I've never really opened myself up but I think I'm ready to.'

Ellie glanced at me, and nodded a small nod before looking down at her trainers again, as I began to tell her a much shorter, concise version of what I'd written down in my diary five years earlier.

Dad's been diagnosed with Leukaemia. Look at that word. Leukaemia.

Now look at it again.

What a horrible looking fucking word.

Who puts an 'a' and an 'e' after a 'k'? What kind of stupid fucking word has letters in that order?

Horrible, ugly, vile looking fucking word.

Mum was already in bits. She knew the symptoms were bad but this bad? He's been suffering from tiredness. Extreme tiredness.

The words were registering with me as we sat but I didn't want them to. And all I can hear is the sound of the ice cream van outside. I'm thinking about being 5 years old and chasing it down the street just as soon as my dad had shoved some coins in my hand and told me not to forget his choc-ice. I looked at him now, sat in his chair and he looked frightened.

He's already ill. And he'll get worse.

He'll get a lot worse.

A moment of quiet as we sat, suddenly broken by Dad's phone alarm going off. As usual, the beep could be heard from 3 continents away. Loud enough so he can hear his alarm reminding him to take his tablets just in case he's in Brazil and has managed to leave his phone at home. The text was from his mobile phone provider, offering him the chance of winning a holiday. Always with the comedy timing.

Weeks later and he's sat up in a hospital bed. His ankles are swollen. His stomach is swollen and he's ballooned to eighteen and a half stone. *'At least I can lend you a pair of my tracksuit bottoms?'* I offered, trying to lighten the mood a bit.

He's taking tablets that make him wee about 20 times a day and is finding it exhausting, walking barefoot back and forth through the ward during the night. Mum is giving me daily urination updates.

'He got up at 4 o'clock this morning and went in his slippers'

I think I knew what she meant.

I also let her off when she tells me that the doctors took his temperature this morning by putting a thermostat in his ear.

He's now pretty unresponsive.

Dropping in and out of consciousness as the chemotherapy takes a firm, firm hold of him, making him sicker and sicker. I seem to be surrounded by stories of sickness and disease. I browse an article in a waiting room saying toast can cause cancer, just as the hospital radio starts playing 'Life' by Des'ree who is warbling that she'd rather have a piece of toast than see a ghost and now I don't know who or what to believe.

The chemotherapy is to be stopped. He's too weak to take it now. They may also have to stop the blood transfusions.

He's dying.

Responsive days are very few and far between. But tonight, he's sat up. A lady enters, holding tomorrow's menu. The highlight of anyone visiting in a hospital when the chat is starting to wane. We're all tired. But how bad do us visitors look when the lady with the menu asks *'right, who's this for?'*. It's for the man on the hospital bed with tubes up his nose, his t-shirt on back to front and the four classic Bold stains down it. Egg, sweat, blood and gravy. *'It's for my dad'*, I say, pointing at him.

We're waiting alongside another lady in yet another waiting room. Maybe 80 years old.

'Oh, Dr Yeung is lovely isn't she. Is she full foreign or half and half? A lot of them are foreign now aren't they. I'm always getting told off by my niece for saying that and that I need to be more what is it, politics correct? But we're from a different era aren't we'

Yes. A more racist era.

Dr Yeung eventually strode in. Very smart and a very expressive face. She explained the situation to us as honestly as we wanted this kind of news. But it doesn't matter how honest you want people to be, you'll never be ready for the hammer blow of being told these three words.

End. Of. Life.

Palliative care is now the only choice and Dr Yeung says it could be weeks. Mum pretty much collapsed into me for a hug which was the longest hug we'd ever had. She's mentally and physically exhausted. Dad had managed to tell her he felt more compos mentis one day this week. *'Well don't worry, love, you look fine'*. She's still making me laugh without trying and I need it right now. I return the favour, giving her what I think she needs.

'I took this today, Mum, can you believe that? Outside the hospital as well.'

'That'll be someone looking down on him, Danny. It's so real looking. And over the hospital as well? See, you're not a believer but how do you explain that?'

Two hours earlier, I had Googled and screenshotted *'Clouds in the shape of a white feather'*.

That's how I'm explaining it.

But not to her.

A white feather and an even whiter lie but one I'm willing to do as long as it numbed any pain or grief she was feeling even for the slightest second. Just some kind of bright moment for her. Of course I don't believe in white feathers being guardian angels.

But she did.

And I'm going to do every trick in the fucking book if it makes her feel better.

He's now sleeping 22 hours a day. He looks like a frail giant. During a rare moment of consciousness, he tells Mum *'I'm sorry if I'm being a burden'*. He's still got her wellbeing and thoughts as his priority and it breaks my fucking heart in two.

He refused a Lion Bar tonight for the first time in 30 years. I'm finding myself in a weird realm between not wanting him to linger in pain and suffer but also desperately wanting him to cling on forever. He's my dad. Is there a set way to feel about this? Do people have guilt for wanting it over quickly or for not wanting it over at all? I'll deal with it my own way. Because there's no set way. I'll spend the little time left I have with him and I'll smile. And I won't take any more fucking Lion Bars in.

He's in the hospice. I don't know how long he's got. It's the only answer we all want to know but we are also afraid to ask the question. A consultant named Claire has arrived to discuss the very imminent future. The question we want to ask is still hanging, thickly in the air. There's clearly a massive elephant in the room. Not Claire, I should say, she's lovely.

But I want her to forget, so much. I don't want the truth and suddenly I can't swallow for about ten seconds as she says he might only have a couple of weeks.

Tonight, I leant over to pour some lemon barley water into dad's cup and accidentally pressed the button on the bed that makes the bottom half of the bed move up and down. Dad hadn't been himself for weeks, months... but then he gave me the look that had terrified me since the age of about 8 and I had NEVER been so happy to see it. For a split second, my dad was back in the room. Albeit bollocking me. I drive home, smiling to myself, remembering who he was. Who he is. The extremely serious disciplinarian. But also, the man who once bumped into Fatima Whitbread in a lift, looked at her, panicked, and said 'Hello, Tessa'.

I'm in the office. Smooth FM is playing and its 9:30am. They've already played four tearjerkers and of course, 'Dance with my father' has just come on. I never danced with my dad although I do remember head butting him by accident while playing sponge football in the hall. The only other times I saw him cry happened when I saw a glimpse of a tear as he watched Cilla Black reunite long lost families on Surprise Surprise. He thought I couldn't see him but I could.

I saw a lot.

I think my Mum knew I could see it.

'Hey, Danny's quiet, isn't he?'

'Yeah. He's just taking it all in aren't you, Daniel'

And I was.

Those tears watching Surprise Surprise showed me that he was a bit of a softie beneath that whole sporty, moustachioed, dare I say it, Alpha Male persona.

As Luther Vandross was cut off by an annoying radio DJ, my mobile phone rang. It was the day that my dad died.

The fluid was building up and the death rattle breathing had begun. He was drowning in the air.

Sixty painter and decorators, volunteers from Scotland, were beavering away outside, giving the hospice a makeover. The hospice was looking a lot brighter. Dad's situation wasn't. But it could be days still, I was told. So, I drove home to get a phone charger, which may be the worst decision I've ever made in my life.

And I've made a few.

Of course, I'm the furthest possible distance away from the hospice when my phone rings, so I pull over.

'Danny, you need to come back. Quick.'

Fuck. Fuck. Fuck. Fuck. Fuck. Fuck.

I want to write it a thousand times. A million fucking times. Fuck.

He'd gone.

I drove back to the hospice and don't remember a thing about the drive. Auto pilot. Had I gone through any red lights? Would I have noticed? And I walked in. And I sat. Alone. Me and him.

Looking at him in the way I looked at him after I'd head butted him playing sponge football. In shock. But still in awe.

A peaceful giant.

He'd gone.

He'd gone.

And he looked so fucking peaceful. So fucking peaceful.

And I told him he looked so fucking peaceful.

And then I let out a sob I had never let out before.

'He looked so fucking peaceful, Ellie.'

'Come here. Hey. Come here. It's ok.'

This time I looked up from my own muddy, leafy trainers and looked straight into Ellie's glazed eyes, which mirrored mine. She gave me a hug which I swear lasted the exact same length of time as the hug my Mum had given me when she collapsed into my arms. And I felt safe.

'Come on Danny. Let's walk back.'

Ellie grabbed my hand again, this time even tighter than before and again, she rubbed my thumb with hers.

Fairground

'Spin it up t'side, Darren f'fuck's serk the bastard camel azzent even fuckin moved yet.'

'Am tryin' to, Dad, y'knobhead, shurrup, concentrate on yer own bastard camel.'

The Arabian Derby was getting competitive.

There were already 9 people sat down, myself and Ellie included, wasting pound after pound, furiously trying to grab and throw balls up into different coloured holes as the disinterested sheikh, maybe the first ginger sheikh born and raised in Billinge, spat rapid fire nonsense into his faulty microphone for the 132nd time that morning.

'Great idea for F, Ellie. But now you're going to have to carry a blue two-foot dragon around for the rest of the day.'

'Maybe I shouldn't be so good at The Arabian Derby then, should I? I told you I was competitive. Especially if blue dragons are at stake.'

We walked around and managed to tick off every romantic fairground trope we could think of.

'Come on Ellie, let's pretend we're a couple in one of those films I've never seen which have a random odd number in them like 45 Days of Summer, 29 Things I Don't Like About You and 37 First Dates.'

'They're not the titles.'

'I told you…I haven't seen them…come on it's your turn. Do a romantic cheesy fairground thing.'

So, she went to feed me some candy floss, stuck it to my nose instead and rolled her head back doing a fake laugh. It's one of the reasons I'm falling for her. Her natural love of fun and that I, as a formerly obese male, now have the overwhelming smell of hot sugar funnelling through my nostrils.

'Ghost train!! Come on, Danny!!'

I never really used to be a fan of ghost trains due to my dad tickling my ear, going 'wooooh' and saying it was a spider, thus scaring the living fuck out of an already anxious 7-year-old in the midst of developing arachnophobia and a fear of getting his ears tickled on ghost trains.

But it wasn't going to deter me from squeezing into a car with Ellie. We held hands. This is better. She hasn't tickled my ears once. I lean in to kiss her on the lips just as the car jolts forward and I almost pull off the most sickening head butt of all time.

And just as quickly as the car jolted forward, it stopped suddenly and Ellie almost pulls off the second most sickening head butt of all time. We're stuck. I don't mind though. I looked over to see a man with a microphone.

'Ellie…is that the Billinge sheikh?'

'I think it is you know? How many jobs has he got in here?'

'I'm sure he was selling hot dogs earlier as well. He might be Shaggy off Scooby Doo. Shaggy loved turning into hot dog salesmen or a sheikh when he was getting chased by a…ghost!'

'Oh my God! You might be on to something there.'

We were still motionless. And then our perfect North West fairground attraction employee of the month began to speak. There were no longer sounds of tortured ghouls and horrific, piercing screams emanating from the ghost train speakers. Just the sound of a twenty something young man with a bumfluff moustache who was born and raised near Haydock, barking safety instructions outside the gates of hell.

'Reet, everybody lizzen up. Please r'mern seated. I will repeat. Please. R'mern. Seated. Thazz bin a problem wi' the power and we'll be on ower way in a cuppla minutes, so please r'mern seated.'

Me and Ellie were trying to contain our muffled laughter so as not to further freak out the young boy, sobbing in the car in front of us. I looked at his dad who was just about to put his arm around his terrified son and I KNEW by the look on his face that he was contemplating tickling his ear one more time.

Laney Tatton

Obsessed with sex. As a 22-year-old, I was more than happy with this but I'd never met anyone so confident, sexually or otherwise, in my short life. A filthy talking, horny whirlwind who you really wouldn't take back to your mother. We'd met in work after I took photographs of her team for the office magazine and she'd emailed me asking if I was going on the works night out at the weekend. The following weekend she was screaming like a banshee in my parents living room and then in my own bedroom. Despite my parents being in Torremolinos, I was still convinced they'd hear her.

'I knew you'd be good at that, Danny'...she said after our first time.

Now I'm a very modest person and never brag or boast about things but at this very moment in time, my only thought was *'Would it be disrespectful to high five myself and moonwalk out of my bedroom and into the bathroom to get a flannel.'*

Laney Tatton would demand sex at least three times a day and looking back was probably a sex addict. She was like a female Michael Douglas…and the going got a lot tougher when she broke my banjo string in a club toilet with some over aggressive oral sex. Blood is never a good sign. Wearing white chinos is never a good sign. Blood mixed with a pair of white chinos is absolutely never a good sign and it was time for the tough to get going. The first time I had become the dumper as opposed to the dumpee and also, for the first time in our fleeting, sex fuelled relationship, I could safely say that she didn't take it very well at all.

Games Night

Me and Tom were sat in our usual pub seats, discussing important matters such as *'If you watch Kill Bill volume 1, can you even hear it?'*, *'What possessed someone to make Poltergeist 5?'* and *'If they made a follow up to The Da Vinci Code, could they call it I Know What You Did Last Supper?'*

'I got aroused watching Countdown the other night, Danny.'

'What??'

'Aroused. Not bad me for me that, 7 letters.'

'Oh right, yeah, I'm with you. Aroused. Good one. Speaking of games, have you thought any more about a game's night with Jenny and Ellie?'

'I have, Danny…good letter G choice. I'm starting to like this alphabet dating thing. Yeah, me and Jenny are free on Friday night. Come round…I'm looking forward to meeting Ellie.'

'So, what games have you got? Shall I bring some?'

'Nah, we've got plenty…Scrabble…Pictionary…the kids have got some interactive nonsense as well we can link to the TV. Oh, and the Wii has been under our bed for years if you want to get that out'

'I've still got mine under my bed too. I think my dad's character is still on there. A living avatar memory from the day he tried to make himself look really thin and gave himself a black moustache instead of a grey one. Did they ever bring out Wii Just for Men?'

'Probably not Danny, no. So that's sorted then. Friday…'

'We used to be cooler than this didn't we, Tom? We haven't always

stayed in and played games on a Friday night?'

'Danny. We're almost in our forties and we haven't even been to a lap dancing bar.'

'What about that time in Leeds?'

'No, what happened in Leeds was a black van with pictures of half-naked women emblazoned on the side pulled up, offering to take us to see some strippers. I wanted to go but you said no and there was no way I was jumping in this pervy A Team vehicle to see them on my own. I remember you saying that the real A team were a crack commando unit sent to prison for a crime they didn't commit and if I'd have gone in on my own, I'd have ended up going to prison for trying to touch the crack of a girl who was going commando.'

I LOVE going for a drink with Tom. He always remembers these stories. Ellie was instantly on board with the date plans for letter G.

'I love this idea Danny…I can't wait to meet Tom!!'

'And Jenny.'

'Tom and Jenny? Like the cartoon cat and mouse? Will there be a woman chasing them around with a massive broom as well?'

'Look…just remember…Tom's almost as competitive as you are. '

'Pfft. He's got no chance. I haven't been beaten in a game of Monopoly for 20 years. OK, I've never finished a game of Monopoly for 20 years but it's technically a true statement. AND I think I already know my H date, Danny. How's that for preparation?'

'Preparation H?

Ellie laughed.

'I've got piles of jokes like that.'

'Ok don't push it. Just get yourself prepared for letter H.'

'I'm intrigued.... but come on...let's get our heads together and our competitive faces on and get letter G done first.'

Ellie fitted in perfectly with Tom and Jenny. I always knew she would but it's always a slight worry hoping everyone gets on with each other.

'Thanks for having us over tonight, Jenny...'

'Aw you're welcome, Ellie...you're always welcome here...I love this thing you and Danny are doing, it's a great idea, this whole alphabet dating.'

'I know! We're really enjoying it. So, what's the best date you and Tom have ever been on?'

'Well, I can't think of the best off the top of my head but the worst was definitely going to see Cats the musical. Tom said he spent the entire first half wondering if the cast all had massive scratch poles in their dressing rooms. He's an absolute nightmare sometimes. We went to one of the kids' shows in school and yes, we all know they can be a bit boring but to sit and calculate how many bulbs were used on all the spotlights in the room is just psychopathic behaviour isn't it?'

'What happened was, Ellie...'

'Tom! You don't need to tell her how you worked it out!!'

Ellie laughed and went along with it.

'You see Ellie, there were curtains with long strings on them. So, I took the mean of 20 strings and then multiplied that by the number of rows. Statistically, the calculation was considered acceptable in engineering terms.'

'Tom...you're boring the poor girl to death. I'm sorry Ellie, he gets all weird when there's a games night on...the competitive juices start to flow and he tries to become the most insane person that ever lived.'

Ellie laughed again. *'So, Tom...what about you, do you know what your favourite date with Jenny was?*

'Our first date was the best date. And I've had the idea to re-enact that first date sometime soon, I think that'll be a nice idea, hey, Jen?'

I continued to watch my girlfriend effortlessly fit in with my best friend and his wife. She seemed to like Tom's date idea.

'Re-enact a first date? I like that idea. I think I'll make a note of that...thanks.'

Somehow, me and Ellie managed to lose every game. Pictionary, which underlined my ability to make any drawing look like it could be mistaken for a 4-year-old attempting heart surgery with a wax crayon. Art had never been my thing. At the age of 12, I would spend my time in school, quivering with shame at the potato I was supposed to be drawing, trying to follow instructions and make it look earthy, shadowed and well...arty. Mine looked like Grant Mitchell had been in a skiing accident.

'How did we lose at Scrabble, Danny?!'

'We were 70 points ahead, Ellie! And I'll tell you why we lost at Scrabble. We lost at Scrabble because Tom knows things that people do not know.'

'Ytterbia, Tom?'

'Ytterbia.'

'What in the living FUCK is Ytterbia?'

'Yeah Tom! What in the living FUCK is Ytterbia?'

'Danny. Ellie. I know a plethora of words. Including plethora.

Ytterbia is a substance…I think it's used in alloys or something?
How many points was that one again, Jen?'

'89 points. A last word winner! My clever, handsome husband!!'

'And sexy, remember.'

'My clever, handsome husband!'

I was gutted. Ellie was gutted. We had them on the ropes.
I was convinced my vulva had won it for us. The second V
was on a triple letter and everything.

Not one single victory. But Ellie had passed the best mate
and his wife test with flying colours.

Of course she did…everyone loves her.

*'So, Tom….Jenny…me and Danny are going to a Holistic Health
and Wellbeing Day next Saturday if you both fancy it?'*

'Are we?'.

'It's my choice for H', Ellie whispered.

This split-second diversion gave Tom and Jenny just
enough chance to think on their feet and come up with
an excuse. Holistic Health and Wellbeing Days were one
hundred percent not their thing.

*'Ah Saturday…yeah, no, we erm, can't do Saturday…the kids have
got…'*

And Tom and Jenny spoke at the exact same time.

'Boxing'

'Choir practice'

And then looked at each other. And spoke again. At exactly
the same time.

'Choir practice'

'Boxing'

'Hey, it's ok…I know not everyone's into this kind of thing as much as I am. It's cool. Not as cool as singing and boxing at the same time but it's all good. Maybe some other time. Plus, Tom. you absolutely do not need to address your intellectual health. Ytterbia??'

Tess Sharpe

I'm 24 years old and seeing someone with the most beautiful teeth I've ever seen. Perfect. However, if I thought my dirty talk needed some work, then Tess Sharpe's blew mine out of the water. A fumble in her car, which turned into more than a fumble, leaving us both naked from the waist up. What she said next may have been and may still be the least sexy thing anyone has ever said, as we groped at each other and she gasped *'Ooh. Are you checking for lumps?'*

ARE YOU CHECKING FOR LUMPS? REALLY? FUCKING HELL, TESS.

Tess Sharpe would always insist on a condom being worn during sex. Nothing wrong with that at all, however I did tell her that condoms weren't 100% safe and that a friend had once fallen down the stairs while wearing one.

Holistic Health and Wellbeing Day

My phone peeped. A text.

'Hey Danny. I'm running a bit late but I'll see you there. 1pm right x?'

'Hey…yeah, no worries I'm just on my way. See you in a bit'

'Don't do anything daft if you get there first. Like starting to believe in any of my nonsense x'

'I think my aura is yellow today. Or it might just be that porridge I had this morning.'

'Knob. See you there in about an hour x'

I walked in and gazed around nervously, not really knowing what to do, how to act. Leaflets! I can read some leaflets. I can skim read some leaflets before Ellie turns up.

'Holistic care refers to a method of providing healthcare that considers the entire individual, including their emotional, social, and psychological well-being in addition to their physical health'

Hmm. Do I believe that essential oils and crystals can cure chronic limb pain and obesity? Maybe stopping eating Monster Munch and starting to eat more vegetables is a wiser move? No, Danny. Open minded. You've got to be more open to this, to please Ellie if nothing else.

I got a tap on my shoulder.

'Is it…it is! Sagittarius guy?'

'Oh. Erm, hello.'

'You were in the restaurant. Amalia! You were at the bar. Greatest first date ever, right? You didn't spill a single meatball!'

'Wow! Hi! That's some memory.'

'Yeah, I'm good with faces…and star signs. Obviously. But then that's me. Typical Scorpio. You on your own?'

'Oh, er no, I'm just waiting for Ellie…you know…from Amalia… she should be here soon.'

'Still going strong then! Ok, I'm gonna go and have a mooch around, see who else I can recognise…there's a guy over there and I'm sure I met him 3 years ago…he had risotto if I remember right.'

'Three years ago? Risotto? You're joking, right?'

'Yeah, I'm joking. He had pizza. Listen, I'll see you later, Sagittarius…and say hi to your girlfriend for me.'

Ellie raced in… baseball cap on…baggy jumper…red converse trainers. Is there anything she doesn't look beautiful in?

'Is there anything you don't look beautiful in?'

'Oh, shut up Danny. What's the leaflet?' she said, after giving me a bear hug that someone as dainty as her absolutely shouldn't be able to pull off.

'Oh, it's just something about…erm…medicines that can help me understand my own innate abilities to heal myself. I think.'

'Aww, you're really trying aren't you…you're so cute sometimes when you think rubbing a leaf on your temple means you're not going to get a brain haemorrhage.'

'It's just, you know. There's proper medicine, Ellie. Liquorice doesn't cure deafness.'

'Liquorice does not cure deafness, Danny, no.'

'Sorry. I am trying, honestly.'

'I know. Come on. Let's get you a coffee and get me a milky tea. We'll get some magic holistic sugar as well and rub it on those bunions of yours.'

Ellie looked at me the way I love her looking at me. Like I'm stupid but also like she likes me and wants me to know that she likes me.

It's what we've had ever since we met. A shared humour. A difficult to describe magnifying ability to bring each other's best features to the fore. And a genuine, extremely powerfully charged eye contact that I could not even begin to explain.

Molly Kershaw

I'm 25. Molly Kershaw was the girl who led me to compile a list. 'Mollyisms'. We hit it off instantly and it was her way of thinking that set her apart from anyone else at the time. I sometimes wondered what was going on inside her mind and even today, I still do.

'I love a carvery but I don't really like meat.'

'I always sit at the back of the plane. Well, you never see them reverse into a mountain, do you.'

'Would Stephen Hawking be able to wheel across a packed beach?'

'Is she really a vegetarian? God, she's got four kids as well.'

'I knew a girl called Christine Onions and she was obsessed with moths.'

'Dave Tranton was the best in our class at going red. He said he just had to really push his face into his head.'

'If David Gest has guests staying over, do they stay in the guest room or is that his room?'

'Do you think there were toilets on the Millenium Falcon?'

As mad as a wet hen. Relationship lasted 7 months.

Josie Bevan

Me and Josie would always have a laugh together. She lived with her parents and had a little brother, Harry. Me and Harry would play football games on the PlayStation for HOURS. I messed this one up one Saturday night / Sunday morning. We're playing another massive final...every game was a massive final to a competitive 26-year-old and an even more competitive 12-year-old. Josie Bevan is in her bedroom; Josie Bevan's mum and dad are in their bedroom and the computer version of the World Cup final is on in Harry Bevan's bedroom. We're concentrating...the sound on the TV is down...we're being as quiet as two mice. It's extra time. This is the moment that the ball ricochets of one of Harry Bevan's Argentinian players legs and rolls back to the Argentinian goalkeeper, who proceeds to pick up the ball. Which is also the moment a 26-year-old man in charge of 11 Spanish computer football players decides to stand up in a deathly quiet house and shout *'THAT'S A FUCKING BACKPASS!!!'*

I hear footsteps.

More than one set of footsteps.

I see Josie Bevan standing at the door with her hands on

her hips and I see a much larger figure. Her father, Tony Bevan...standing behind her.

'Get that thing turned off NOW and get to bed, Harry. Danny, I'll phone you a taxi. I expect better from you.'

Fuck.

We split up a couple of weeks later. Not over the computer game, I should add and ironically, neither of us really needed consoling.

And it was definitely a back pass by the way.

Ice Skating

The dates were now coming thick and fast. Once again, Ellie effortlessly wore a bobble hat, ear muffs and a body warmer. I'd only ever seen Natalie Imbruglia and Keira Knightley pull off a bobble hat nearly this well. My own bobble hat made me look like the mad person on the bus who insists on shouting to the driver about baked beans.

But I took the lead…held her hand and laughed as we whizzed around the ice rink…a truly, old fashioned romantic date. Holding hands is always good. Especially with someone who looks this good in a bobble hat.

'I've already got my J sorted, Danny.'

'Already? Ok, can I have a guess? I reckon I know it…there's not many options for J.'

'One guess. That's all.'

'Jacuzzi. A spa day. Who doesn't love a spa day. Got to be.'

'Nope. Although you're kind of close.'

'Kind of close? How can there be another J kind of close to jacuzzi?'

'It's got two letter zeds in it.'

'Oh god…'

Jazz Night

We both walked out during the interval.

'So, we're in agreement, then?'

'Sorry Danny…yeah, it was rubbish. Sorry.'

'But we live to fight another day, right? Another letter?'

'Are you sure you really want to? I messed that one up didn't I.'

'We could have been sat in a jacuzzi, Ellie…'

'We could have been…but then we'd never have heard that man blowing into his trumpetty saxophone thing for forty-five minutes.'

'Were we the only ones not enjoying it? I'm sure everyone else was nodding along and tapping their feet.'

'Snobs, I reckon, Danny. They'd lose their mind if they ever heard Livin' On A Prayer.'

Jess Bracken

At the age of 28, Jess Bracken almost broke my penis. There I said it. Her house was amazing. I remember walking into her bathroom, looking at the huge ornate bath and thinking 'I could overrun that and eat a Flake in there'. Her bedroom was just as welcoming. Crisp, white virginal bedsheets and possibly my first ever experience of scatter cushions.

Jess Bracken proceeded to substitute my penis for a bottle of tomato sauce and started manhandling it and yanking it for all it was worth. A foreskin has never been pulled back this far in the history of foreskins. It was like someone struggling to get a pepperami out of its meaty sheath. I looked down. More blood. The white virginal sheets now had a touch of Nightmare on Elm Street 3, Dream Warriors about them. I looked down at my bloody member which was now beginning to look like Rocky Balboa in the 12th round against Ivan Drago and I almost passed out. What has happened there then, Danny? I said to myself.

Your knob looks like it's about to go on a 12-hour long haul flight and has rested itself on one of those pink sleeping cushions. There was what looked like an inflatable ring around my helmet. It doesn't look right at all and it looked even worse the following day, when I turned up at the hospital to get it looked at.

A Doctor Humphries was about to see it in all its glory.

'Right then, let's have a look. What have we got?'

What I wanted to say was *'Well Doctor Humphries, what we've got is the fact that Jess Bracken, as lovely as she is, as lovely as her bathroom is and as lovely as her scatter cushions are, has managed to make my penis look like Sloth from The Goonies going to a fancy-dress party as John Merrick.'*

But I didn't. I just dropped my pants. Watched Doctor Humphries pull a face which said *'Yeah, I see about 13 of these Sloth Merricks every day'*, watched him go to the fridge, pull out some ice and then slowly but surely, like Demi Moore and Patrick Swayze building a foreskin vase, slowly pull it up and back into its rightful position. I've never wanted to hug another man so much in my life.

Donna McDowall

I'm 30 years old and have been introduced to Donna McDowall by her brother, who I met on a stag do. His stag do. I was invited along by a close-ish friend, so I got involved as best as possible and did the whole tiresome stag do thing. I wore a tee-shirt with the stag's face on it and got a problematic, offensive nickname printed on the back of it. I spoke awkwardly with people I didn't really know and I watched someone drink out of a shoe. All of the things I would choose not to do on a night out. I kept the tee-shirt as one of those *'it's cold in bed tonight, I'll stick that in my drawer'* tee shirts with the other *'it's cold in bed tonight, I'll stick that in my drawer'* tee-shirts.

Donna McDowall had stayed over one frosty evening and as we woke, slightly hungover, we began a pre-toothpaste kiss and fumble which led to the inevitable. Until thirty seconds into the excitement, Donna McDowall asked if we could stop.

'Danny…can we stop?'

'Are you ok? What's up? Shall I go and brush my teeth?'

'No, can you take your tee-shirt off please?'

'Yeah, what's up?'

'I don't want to look at my brother's face while we're having sex.'

Karaoke

'Woooooah we're half way therrrrre, woooahhh-oahh livin' on a prayerrrr!!! Take my hand and we'll make it up squarrrreee, woooaaahhh-ohhh living on a prayer!!!'

I stumbled off stage and straight into a high five and a hug off Ellie.

'Yaaayyyyy!! I loved it! Couple of questions though.'

'Questions?', I replied, out of breath.

'We'll make it up square? Did you sing 'we'll make it up square?'

'Yeah, the lyrics...we'll make it up squaaaarreeee.'

'It's we'll make it, I swear. It even said those words on the lyrics plastered on those 4 screens around the pub.'

'That makes more sense to be honest. I've been getting that wrong for years.'

'Aww don't worry, we'll get you put in a home with Jon Bon Jovi and the rest of them. You can all sit around and eat soup together.'

'Hey Ellie, did you know Jon Bon Jovi met the rest of his band mates when they worked at the fair?'

'.... go on...'

'Tommy used to work on the ducks.'

Thankfully, the silence was broken by a man with a microphone, wearing a Hawaiian shirt and adorning massive Elton John style glasses in order to substitute a lack of actual personality.

'Next up we've got Ellieeee, where's Ellie?'

Ellie looked at me nervously…why is there apprehension in her eyes? Is she the worst singer of all time? Oh god, it could be even worse. She might be an amazing singer and there's nothing worse than an amazing singer showing off at Karaoke. Or it could be even worse than that. She might have put her name down to sing Dancing in the Moonlight. That would be it. We've had a good run. We got to letter K. But Toploader would be a step too far.

Ellie started to sing. Her body language was strangely quiet for someone so seemingly extroverted. Looking at her feet and shuffling slightly from side to side.

'I get up in the evenin'. And I ain't got nothing to say.

I come home in the mornin. I go to bed feelin the same way

I ain't nothing but tired. Man, I'm just tired and bored with myself

And then she looked up. Directly at me.

'Hey there baby. I could use just a little help…'

And a bolt of excitement shot through my body. Maybe a vulnerability I'd not really seen in Ellie before? Was it because she was singing Bruce Springsteen? Was it the fact that she fitted slap bang in the middle of the karaoke person who either wails like a banshee down the microphone and the person that knows they can sing and all of a sudden, turns into Celine Dion in their own head? Was it because I thought I was about to be pulled up on stage like Courteney Cox? It was the vulnerability. And the modesty. Fuck.

'There's somethin' happenin' somewhere…

Baby I just know that there is…. you can't start a fire…you can't start a fire without a spark…'

She was still making direct eye contact with me and I forgot there was anyone or anything else in the pub.

'That was Elllieeeee, everyone, another round of applause for Ellieeee.'

Ellie flicked her hair out of her eyes and made a small jump down off the stage, started looking down at her feet again, before striding over, looking back up at me and straight into my high five, kiss and bear hug.

I spun her around twice.

'That was brilliant! You can sing!'

'Aw, thanks. Did you feel like Courteney Cox?'

'There's never a moment in life when I don't feel like Courteney Cox. No honestly, that was AMAZING. I don't think I'll ever forget that. Two more beers?'

'Get me a shot, too. I'm shaking.'

'Two beers and two shots. I'm putting my name down again.'

Four beers and four shots later, we were sat, open mouthed at the man at the bar, who was wearing a leather jacket with Al Pacino as Scarface emblazoned on the back.

'Let's hear it again for Adammmmm!!!'

Adam, a friend of Tony Montana's over at the bar had just performed 500 miles by The Proclaimers, which is why me and Ellie were now sitting down slightly out of breath.

Next up its Danny again! Singing Kiss Me! Come on Danny!'

'Yayyyyy Danny! Don't forget to get the words right this time. The screens, remember.'

'Yeah, yeah, you're the boss.'

'Was that a Bruce Springsteen joke?'

It was my turn to give Ellie a knowing look, a smile and a quick kiss, before turning, standing up and stumbling up the stairs to take the microphone off a man who was now holding an inflatable saxophone and wearing a possibly offensive Scottish wig.

'If we could take a photo…eternalize this moment…

…for the days when I don't believe'

No one in the pub knew the song but I'd heard it recently and something resonated with me. How I felt about Ellie.

It was my turn to look up as I continued to absolutely murder a song I was beginning to love and a lyric I was beginning to love even more.

'…let this night invade my lungs, you're all I want to breathe…

…right beside the lake, I burned for you…you burned for me… So, kiss me the way…that you would if we died tonight…

And hold me the way that you would for the final time…'

'That was Danny! Round of applause for Danny, good effort!'

Ellie was drowning out the silence with whistling, whooping and applause.

'I loved that! I've never heard the song before.VERY romantic.'
And she started to sing it herself, back to me. But better.
'…right beside the lake, I burned for you…you burned for me…

…So, kiss me the way…that you would if we died tonight.

Hold me the way that you would for the final time'

And we kissed. And inwardly, I prayed that it wasn't for the final time.

'I've got my letter L, Danny. You've just made the decision for me'

Ellie walked to the bar and I could just about hear her singing again... *'right beside the lake, I burned for you, you burned for me...'*

The Lake

Tom brought the usual over to our table. Two pints. Salted peanuts.

'You ok, Danny? You're quiet. Wait! You're not still mad about Ytterbia are you?'

'No... I'm just thinking about the weekend...this is the first time we'll have been away for more than a couple of nights and you know what my track record is like.'

'Thank God for that, I thought you were still angry about Scrabble. You could always go to anger management? I've heard it's all the rage.'

'I'm serious, Tom. I don't want to mess this up. I really like her. I mean, REALLY like her.'

'So where are you going for letter L?'

'Well, it's the lake...but we're going to a 'hideaway'. Just a cabin... pretty remote, no other people. Me. Ellie. Nature.'

'Sounds like heaven.'

'Man versus nature. Although we get given a load of meat for our barbecue...I can take control of that...she's picked the venue...I'll be the hunter gatherer.'

'You're like Bear Grylls basically, Danny. You'll be fine. Be like Bear. He's always positive. His glass always seems to be half full. Half full of his own piss, admittedly but still.'

I had nothing to worry about. The hideaway was perfect. And I managed to say the three words I had struggled with for years as they'd sometimes feel empty or forced. But not as we sat, laughing and talking by the lake. I moved her windswept hair, revealing the deep green, manga eyes and knew the time was right.

'I love you, Ellie.'

'I love you too, Danny.'

Ellie kept her eye contact and then looked down again, smiling. It was this fragility and vulnerability that would appear from nowhere that I couldn't understand. For someone so extrovert, funny and confident, it really confused me. But I stayed quiet, not wanting to spoil what was a perfect moment. Instead, I pulled her in close from the waist, kissed her and held her, before releasing her and bending down to stoke our fire a bit and blowing on it, pretending to know what I was doing.

Bear Grylls and his half full glass of optimistic piss would have been proud of me.

The following morning, as we drove away from the hideaway and out of the countryside, we spotted a potential future date venue. Well, Ellie did.

'Danny, look at that sign! X-Treme Sports! Who's turn will it be for X? That HAS to be our X date.'

My first thought was *'She wants to go to X… that's about ten dates away. More than ten dates away? She wants at least another ten dates with me.'*

My second thought was *'Danny, she told you she loved you less than 24 hours ago. Stop doubting yourself and being pessimistic. Bear Grylls, remember. Half full glasses of optimistic piss.'*

I turned to Ellie and nodded. *'Yep, that's got to be the X. It's*

going to be your choice as well and at least it means you don't have
to find xylophone lessons for us. The jazz night was bad enough.

'That's sorted then. It's a date. A future date.'

We both smiled at each other, hit shuffle on a Spotify
playlist and continued the long drive home, absolutely
nailing a version of Dead Ringer for Love by Meatloaf and
Cher.

Andrea Cassini

I'm 32 and casually seeing an Italian girl, which, when I
tell people, instantly makes me a stud. Because history
and popular culture tells us that all Italian women are
stunningly beautiful and have massive eyes like a Dolmio
puppet.

What history and popular culture doesn't tell us is that
some Italian girls are into a bit of light bondage involving
Italian football kits. Well, Andrea Cassini was.

In the throes of passion one night, she asked me to tie her
hands to the headboard. She was already wearing my AC
Milan football top; A present she had bought me. Despite
working on a DIY section of a well-known department
store many years ago, I didn't have any kind of 'tying up'
equipment to hand. What I did have however, was a pair
of AC Milan football socks, which Andrea Cassini had also
bought me and a basic boy scout knowledge of sexy knots.

So, I proceeded to make sure Andrea Cassini was
comfortably secured and tied to the bed and... well...we
continued with the throes of passion.

'Do me, do me...do me...' was the muffled cry as the Dolmio

puppet eyes looked up at me.

Yes, Danny. You ARE the man. Until I heard the fourth *'do me'*…which wasn't as muffled. And it had another syllable at the start. *'Undo me....undo me...'* Oh shit. Nothing breaks a moment of passion more than someone panting *'My wrist! It's too tight!'*

I panicked…and all of a sudden had forgotten the lesson at boy scouts where we were taught to undo Italian football sock sex knots, which led me to start pulling at them, making things even worse.

It lasted around a year. The relationship…not the time it took me to untie her and still, to this day, I wince when I see an advert for Dolmio, thinking that the Mafia head of the felt family is going to tie a puppet horse head to my headboard.

Movie Night

I'd been waiting to show Ellie the second film in the trilogy. It was Tuesday night, quite late and I reached for my phone and began to text.

'Hey Ellie. You ready for M?'

'Hey! I've been waiting for ages for this…don't leave me hanging. What is it? x'

'It's…a movie night.'

'Yes! What are we going to see? x'

'Well, Julie Delpy…Ethan Hawke here would like to take you on a date to see Before Sunset.'

'Jesse and Celine! At last! Is this why you said I wasn't allowed to watch it after we saw the first one? Sneaky, Danny…sneaky. But I like your style x'

'It's showing this weekend. I've got the tickets.'

'Awww…Can't wait. We can act out the scenes again x'

We were completely silent for 80 minutes. I'd grab Ellie's hand and it put it on my knee. Ellie would squeeze my knee then place my hand on hers. I'd grab her hand and place it on my lap and hold on to it with both hands. We were totally immersed in the film, watching a couple's love story play out, mirroring our own.

'One black coffee, one milky tea and that massive slab of carrot cake please. And can I have two forks as well, thanks.'

I was sharing cake. I told you I loved her.

'Dannnyyyyyy....it's US!! It's still US!!! Ok, Jesse's married and Celine has a boyfriend but they're MADE for each other aren't they! Oh my god when can we watch the last one?'

'I knew you'd like it.' I handed Ellie a fork and she tucked in, excitedly relaying the film in between mouthfuls of carrot cake.

'He's not happy with his relationship. She's not happy with her relationship. It's too common. Why do people settle with a relationship they're not happy in?'

'I know...it's happened to me in the past. I think being alone and happy is better than being with someone but feeling lonely.'

'If we ever get that way, we'll tell each other, right?'

'Right.'

'Ok...rules are rules, Danny. I think I know which part of the film I want to re-enact.'

'I think I know, too. The astrology bit, right? It has to be.'

'You know me so well. You ready?'

'I'm ready...can I do the American accent?'

'Your last one sounded like Harold Bishop.'

'Ok, I'll use my normal voice.'

Ellie turned her phone on and found the quotes website, the same as she had done after our letter C Cinema date. She sent me the link.

'Ok you're first, Danny. Ready? Aaaand action.'

'Do you believe in, like... ghosts or spirits?'

'Uhm, no.'

'No?'

'No.'

'Ok, what about reincarnation?'

'Not at all.'

'God?'

'No. That sounds... that sounds terrible. No, no, no. But, at the same time I don't want to be one of those people that don't believe in any kind of magic, you know?'

'So then, astrology?'

'Yes, of course!'

'There we go, right!'

'I mean, that makes sense, right? You're a Scorpio, I'm a Sagittarius, so we get along.'

I knew Ellie was invested in the film but as soon as this scene played out, she squoze my hand tighter than she ever had. Julie Delpy merely saying the word Sagittarius induced a vice like grip on my knee.

'Can we do another bit? That bit we were laughing at?'

'The spanking bit?'

'The spanking bit!'

'Sure...send me the quotes and I'll get back into character.'

'Ok one sec.'

'Ok looks like you're first this time. Aaandd...'

'Hang on, take the last piece of cake first...'

'Thanks...ok...aaaand ACTION!'

Ellie began to read the dialogue from the script.

'Anyway, this friend of mine, she was telling me that next time she dates another man, she's gonna make a little questionnaire, about what they like and dislike, before they even...'

'Oh, like written down, or out loud?'

'Yeah, yeah, written down, mostly written down. But it wouldn't be just... you know, yes or no, it would be a little more complex than that. Like for example, if the question is: Are you into S&M? The answer could be, no, but, a good spanking once in a while doesn't hurt.'

We both laughed again.

I wanted to carry on reading dialogue from the film, with someone I wanted to create and tell more and more stories similar to those of Jesse's and Celine's.

But Ellie was already moving forwards.

'My turn next, Danny. Letter N. You've got a job to do. Pick a nice bottle of wine for us.'

'Ok I'm on it. What's the plan?'

'Just a night in. Me and you.'

'Perfect.'

Night In

The bottle of wine had turned into a second one quite quickly. After our romantic nights at the lake and our movie night, the level of comfort between me and Ellie had turned up a notch. It was easy now. Awkward silences were a thing of the past and actual silences were welcomed if anything...no need to fill the air with needless talk.

Bigger plans we're also being discussed.

'Ellie...I know we're only doing letter N tonight but I've already kind of got a letter S planned...but you'll need to take a couple of weeks off work sometime in the next couple of months. I've bought you something as a clue...I've started reading it but I think you'll like it too, so I got you a copy...it's about spirituality...and travel. Right up your street.'

'Aww thanks Danny. You know I love gifts. You're always so good with your gifts.'

Ellie ripped the wrapping paper. The way presents should be opened. None of this dainty, gentle opening of a present and then folding the paper neatly in a pile. Rip and throw. She was a rip and thrower.

'The Pilgrimage! Paulo Coelho. I've heard of this guy! He wrote The Alchemist, right?'

'That's him. It's about a religious walk he did. El Camino de Santiago.'

'And we're doing the walk!? How long does it take?'

'Well, we can't do the whole thing. It's about 35 days...but I've

looked into it a little bit and we can maybe start around half way and walk into...letter S... Santiago?'

'Really! Santiago!! Oh my God, Danny. I love this. I need to ramp up my dating game.'

'It doesn't matter where we go, Ellie. As long as we go together. Skegness. Scarborough. Santiago. It's all the same to me. I'm really going to try harder this time. You know, with the spirituality and all that. Maybe this book is what I need to give me a little nudge?'

'Maybe it is, Danny. Just give it a go, what harm will it do. Hey did you say your Mum was into spirituality. And horoscopes? I'm sure you mentioned she was spiritual? Wasn't she into white feathers?'

'I don't think horoscopes were her thing. White feathers, definitely. She thought it was a gift...the gift of a guardian angel watching over her. Normally my grandma or my grandad. She'd spot them more if she was feeling down for any reason.'

'How do you feel about them yourself?'

'I notice them more, now that she's gone. They remind me of her if anything and it gives me a nice feeling if I see one.'

'That's nice, Danny. I think that can help. You ok?'

The second bottle of wine had kicked in. It must have been a 1965 Chateau Neuf du Melancholy. I was excited by Ellie's reaction to the Santiago idea but it was mixed with a wave of sadness flowing through me again just by talking about my Mum. Something I was happy to do. But usually on my terms...and this, tonight, had hit me suddenly.

'Come on...come here...it's fine.'

Ellie rubbed a solitary tear that was falling from my cheek as if I'd just sang Sinead's beautiful *'All the flowers that you planted, Mama, in the back yard...all died when you went away.'*

lyric.

She held me closer.

It had been three years.

Three years since my heart had been destroyed and I'd let out a sob I had only ever let out once before.

And for the second time, I told Ellie a much more condensed version of what I had written in my diary three years previously.

Life is so fucking hard sometimes. No one tells you that it's supposed to be hard. If we didn't suffer, then we wouldn't learn. But sometimes I don't want to learn. I just want to hear her voice again.

I lost my Mum this morning.

The last time I lost her was in Sainsbury's. I was 5 years old and it was terrifying. This time I've lost her for good. But this time I'm not so scared.

She was the best Mum in the world and the best Nan in the world. She even had two cups to prove it.

She never complained about her illness once and maintained her compassion and empathy for others like no one or nothing I have ever seen before. An unbreakable will to enjoy life, combined with an unrelenting love and passion for her family and others.

I don't know if anyone will ever read this but if you've lost your Mum, my broken heart goes out to you.

I don't know if anyone will ever read this but if you are a Mum, keep doing what you're doing. You deserve that cup in your cupboard.

And if you do read this, please don't tell anyone else I wrote it. It's just for you. Keep mum.

For as long as you can.

Breast cancer. An operation. The all clear. Then the return of the disease. The return with a fucking vengeance.

A nurse who had been looking after her for months broke the news. *'There's nothing else we can do now. I'm sorry. I'm so sorry.'*

And my Mum held out her arms to the nurse, brought her in towards her, hugged her tightly, kissed her cheek and said *'Thank you for everything you've done. I know you've done all you can.'*

And my own outlook on life changed right there and then.

Watching someone react that way to being given the worst possible news filled me with a pride for the person I loved more than I have ever loved anyone in my life and I watched on, with my own heart shattered into a thousand pieces, witnessing what seemed like life taking place in an alternate dimension, as a healthy nurse stood, in tears, being consoled by a lady with weeks, maybe days left to live.

And I vowed from that moment to be better. To help people. To be nice to people. An absolute non-negotiable. Nothing else matters.

Nothing. Else. Matters.

'You'll never get dizzy doing good turns, Daniel', my Mum would always say.

But this time there were no angels. No white feathers. No signs. It was all too real. And a massive part of me died inside when she said her last goodbye.

Mum always used to say Wednesday was a bad day.
Because payday for her and my dad was on a Thursday.

She died on a Wednesday.

And I all I wanted was for her to come back from the shops
on Thursday so I could have two fig rolls and a penguin for
my supper.

No angels. No white feathers. No signs. All too real.

I didn't cry much.

I haven't cried much.

But I am inconsolable right now as I sit and write this.

The tears will arrive if I'm at the grave and phone my
Auntie to tell her where I am.

'Tell her that I miss her, Danny.'

And that's when I crumble.

*'...And that's when I crumble, Ellie. When someone tells me that
they miss her. Because it reminds me, I do, too. Every day. And some
days...some days I forget what her voice sounded like and those
days kill me. Once in a while, when I wake up, I'll lie there for
about five seconds, trying to remember the dream I've just had. A
feeling that I've lost something. Someone. And I'm always searching
for something, somewhere, someone to help me understand. When
it's really cold and I can't feel a thing, I'd like to die...but then I
remember the warmth. Her warmth. Picking me up time after time.
A grazed knee? She picks me up. I feel like I'm failing in life? She
picks me up. I'm down...down for whatever reason? She picks me up.
I need advice? She advises me. And picks me up. She always picks.
me. up.'*

Again, Ellie's glazed eyes mirrored my own and we stared at each other, silently, before she smiled at me, reassuringly. She hugged me and wiped another tear from my cheek.

'You're doing great, Danny. Come on, lets finish these drinks and head to bed. Hey…look at me…you're doing great. Keep talking about her. Every day if you need to.'

'She died on the 24th of July, Ellie.

24/7.

You'll like that. You like the thing with numbers. I get to think about her 24/7.'

'Yeah, you do. And you should. Come on Danny, I'll turn the lights off.'

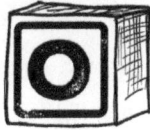

Out Out

Me and Tom were sat in our favourite corner of the pub.

'What's up Tom? Something's up.'

'It's our Jamie. He's had his exam results and he didn't get what he wanted.'

'We didn't do too well on ours and we turned out alright, didn't we? Tell him not to worry about it.'

'Yeah, I know but you know what kids are like, they put themselves under so much pressure. I worry about him that's all.'

'Look at Brian Harvey.'

'What?'

'Brian Harvey from East 17.'

'What about Brian Harvey from East 17?'

'He got 9 A's and a B and ended up running himself over after eating too many potatoes. Tell him not to worry.'

'Cheers Danny. That's…helpful…'

'Happy to help. You know me. He's only a kid. Tell him one of those quotes people like on social media to motivate him. Tell him to do something every day that scares him.'

'Right. So, tell me, when was the last time YOU did something that scared YOU?'

'The other week when I had two pickled eggs, a full packet of Bakewell tarts and three cans of Monster in work and almost followed through on the way home.'

'Yeah, it's hardly motivational life advice though is it, Danny. Anyway, listen, when's this big night out with Ellie?'

'Sunday. Roast dinner booked for 1pm... then I'm taking her out into town. Drinking and dancing. It's going really well...there's the Santiago thing I told you about and we had a chat about my Mum the other night...she goes in a bit too hard on the spiritual stuff sometimes but I know she means well...'

'Yeah, course she does. It's just her way of dealing with things probably...just go out and enjoy Sunday...and hopefully they'll have some East 17 playing for you somewhere. Just make sure you take it easy on the roast potatoes.'

It's 9pm. I've got mint sauce on my shirt and I'm about to monumentally fuck things up. Why press the self-destruct button when you've met someone who could be the one? Why suggest going out so early?

Why did you buy those shots at 4pm?

Why didn't you realise your mood was low? Why did you go drinking on the 24th of July?

'Aww Danny, your Mum would have loved it in here I reckon...all this music. She loved all this old stuff didn't you say? Hey, imagine a white feather was to come down now and land near you.'

She's being nice. Why can't you recognise she's being nice. Look at her eyes. Look at her smile. Don't fuck things up, Danny. Say the second thing that comes into your head you fucking idiot.

Too late.

'Fucks sake Ellie, can't we just have one night without talking about all this white feather, spiritual shit? People are born and people die. I've seen it. Fuck me, I've seen it. Twice.Why can't people

*just get it? There aren't any fucking magic angels out there. Stop
living this floaty bullshit nonsense and wake up. Just because
you've woken up at 3:33am or 4:44am or 5 fifty fucking five am
doesn't mean angels are watching over you and making sure you're
ok.*

THEY'RE FUCKING NUMBERS.

LIFE. ISN'T. A. FUCKING. GAME.'

Ellie froze.

And a tear began to form in the corner of her eye. That
same corner of her eye that a tear appeared when she
listened to me talk about my dad dying. That same corner
of her eye when she listened to me talk about my mum
dying. And as she always did when she felt uncomfortable
or scared, she looked down. Down at her feet. But this
time she didn't look back up. She turned…she turned away
and walked towards the door…and I stood motionless.
What do I do? What have I done? I've upset the one person
who has stood by me and I've shouted the words *'LIFE.
ISN'T. A. FUCKING. GAME'*…while asking her to pick dates
based on a letter of the fucking alphabet? You, Danny.
You're the one playing a fucking game.

I ran outside but it was too late.

Her taxi was already pulling away and all I could see was a
bowed head. Ellie was still looking at her shoes…but had
her head in her hands.

Well done, Danny. Fucking idiot.

Fuck you.

Back to letter A.

Actually, no, don't even fucking bother.

79

We'd never gone more than 24 hours without any contact.

I've fucked it up. I've fucked it all up. What do I say?

Day 4 and I've typed out and deleted at least thirteen messages, trying to get the words right. Just be honest. Eventually, I managed to text how I felt.

'I'm so sorry. I didn't mean any of what I said. Everything got on top of me. I'm sorry. X'

Ellie was usually a quick replier. Not this time. 10 minutes. Nothing. Half an hour. Nothing.

Fuck. I've fucked it all up. An hour. Nothing.

Two hours. Three hours.

My phone peeped.

It was Ellie's peep.

I didn't want to open the message and just stared at the phone like a bomb disposal expert making sure he'd picked the right wire, or even worse, like someone in Tesco Express painstakingly trying to decide which fucking meal deal sandwich to pick up. I eventually plucked up the courage, pulled myself together and opened it. What's the worst that could happen. I could always start again at A with someone else. It's not the end of the world.

Fuck off, Danny. Right now, it is the end of the world. I opened the message.

'You really hurt me, Danny. You really upset me. I've thought long and hard about us. And a next date. It's my turn for letter P, right? x'

My heart almost burst. How does she always know what to say.

'I'm so sorry, Ellie. I'll go anywhere. I fucked up. I know I fucked up x'

'You did fuck up. See you next Tuesday x'

Poetry Writing

'You almost fucked that right up, Danny.'

'Tell me about it, Tom. I don't deserve her. I just get a bit, you know, angry sometimes when people come across too blasé about things close to my heart. Like the other day, someone used the word 'cancerverssary' and I know it's an amazing thing that someone's beaten the disease and is one, two, five, twenty years free of it but 'cancerverssary?' Really? It's too much of a celebratory word. What do you do at these cancerverssary parties, put a blindfold on and start whacking a pinata full of tumours?'

'Wow…ok…for one, yes you do deserve Ellie. Don't put yourself down. You just need to maybe learn to take a breath when people are talking about death, perhaps?

'You're right. I think I'm more afraid of life than I am of death.'

'Very profound, Danny. You definitely read that somewhere online… look, you and Ellie have got something…but you're like a cat sometimes.'

'You mean I've lost another of my nine lives but I've been given another chance?'

'No, I mean you bury your shit in other people's gardens, yes, of course I mean you've been given another chance. You need to relax more, Danny…maybe start meditating or something? Start being a bit more…spiritual? Open your eyes and mind up to stuff a bit more and relax? Be like Ellie.'

'Meditation? Yeah, I might give that a go. It beats sitting around doing nothing.'

'So, letter P? Is it tomorrow, the poetry writing thing?'

'Yeah 6 o'clock start. She was thinking of picking a psychic night at first but it got cancelled...'

'...unforeseen circumstances?'

'Unforeseen circumstances.'

Me and Tom gave each other a knowing look. The kind of look that two friends who have told the same rubbish jokes to each other for more than twenty years give each other.

6pm. Me and Ellie are sat next to each other in a room full of people.

An impressive array of brown clothes filled the room. A man named Colin Henson, with a black, wiry, bouffant hairstyle, an impressive handlebar moustache, a tweed jacket, small round glasses and odd coloured socks gives us all a notepad, a pen AND a pencil.

We were happy.

The atmosphere between me and Ellie had eased as the night had gone on...but the elephant in the room, my fucking stupidity, was still peering its head around the Blue Peter studio and waiting for John Noakes to stroll in and slide arse over tit on the huge mound of argumentative shit that I'd created over a week ago.

'Ok my lovely new poets...you've got two more tasks this evening...I want you to write a short poem about something memorable that happened to you in the last five years and something a little bit longer that has happened to you in the last two weeks. It can be about anything. AND you get to read it out to everyone...I know it's the first time here for a couple of you tonight but you all look confident enough and you've been scribbling away for most of the night.'

'Five years ago?!'

'What are you gonna write about, Danny?'

'God knows. A lot happened in the last five years. What about you?'

'No idea. Let's just write about something daft that we remember. Hey, what about that New Zealand museum experience you told me about. When it was dead quiet in there and you heard someone fart?'

'It's hardly Keats is it. I can't use toilet humour in my first public poetry reading. That's like me asking you to write one about when that lad went for a dump in a unisex toilet.'

'Well, that's made my mind up. Thanks Danny. Pass me that pencil please, mine's broken.'

We got to work. Ellie was finished in no time.

'How've you finished yours so quickly?'

'I'm a natural. And I'm competitive, remember? I've already started my second poem.'

'Second poem?'

'Yeah, you've got to write about something that's happened in the last couple of weeks too.'

'Oh, shit yeah. Best crack on. Shush…stop distracting me.'

The words 'Stop distracting me' were Ellie's cue to start prodding me in the ear with her pencil. MY pencil.

'Hey Danny, do you remember that poem people used to say in school? My friend Billy?'

'Do you mean My friend Billy had a ten-foot willy, he showed it to the girl next door?'

We said the last line in unison.

'She thought it was a snake, so she hit it with a rake and now it's only four foot four!!!'

We both started laughing.

'Yeah, I don't think we can stand up and do that one either, as lovely a duet as it would be. First of all, its plagiarism. And secondly, I don't want to over impress our fellow writers here with our knowledge about a tale of a young lad whose gargantuan penis gets mistaken for a dangerous reptile and subsequently attacked with a garden tool.'

Ellie laughed even more.

Colin Henson called time on our scribbling and asked some of the more established members of the class to stand up and read their first poem. None of which were about farting in a New Zealand museum or someone going for a dump in a unisex toilet, believe it or not.

A shy looking blonde-haired man in his early twenties stood up first and told of his first love. His current love… who he had been sat with all evening.

'Hi…erm…this one's about Katie, over there. She's wrote a poem about pigeons. I've wrote this one about her. Well, about us.

'The Prime of our Lives'

I was 19

She was 17

We met on the corner of 23rd and 31st Not far from the 7-11

We were in the prime of our lives

It was all very odd

'That was lovely, Stewart! Round of applause for Stewart there. So, I think...Katie! You're next up'

Katie walked to the front of the room, held her notebook out and peered over her glasses. She looked like a cross between the two female members of the Scooby Doo gang, managing to look both beautiful and nerdy at once. A lovely quality. The one perfected by Sandra Bullock in every film she's ever appeared in.

Keeping in synch with the rest of the gang from the Mystery Machine, her voice sounded like a cross between Scooby Doo's and Shaggy's as she read out the quite bold and brazen, yet kooky sounding title.

'That's Chewing Gum, You Tit'

Stupid fucking pigeon

Haven't you learned your lesson?

Three times you've approached it

Haven't you learned your lesson?

That's chewing gum, you tit

Bread doesn't smell like mints

Colin Henson looked over his glasses and raised an inquisitive eyebrow. Then looked at me. I looked back at Colin Henson and didn't blink, choosing to just shrug my shoulders at him. We were both in awe at what was either the greatest thing ever written about pigeons or the mumblings of a mad woman. I think it was the former. Katie's boyfriend gave her a supportive round of applause and whispered to the woman sat next to him *'she loves pigeons really, this one just really annoyed her.'* and I knew there and then I was amongst people I liked.

Colin Henson had finally stopped peering over his glasses and called out my name.

'Danny, you're up next...then we'll have Ellie. You can read your poems out after each other so you don't feel too isolated...we're nice to our newbies like that.'

I coughed slightly and cleared my throat.

'This is called 'You Farted in a New Zealand Museum''

Colin Henson looked over his glasses again.

'You Farted in a New Zealand Museum'

Silence broken by a massive clap

Arse applause by the Māori weapons

Weapons that were silent. But deadly

A sharp, vile gust

A reverberating quacker

To be heard from near the rugby display

And enough to halt a haka

Ellie started laughing and started the slow ripple of applause and odd giggle around the room.

'Ok Ellie, your turn please.'

'Thanks Mr Henson.'

'Colin...please.'

'Thanks Colin. Erm this one's called 'Should you go for a dump in a unisex toilet?'

Colin Henson let out a slight sigh and rubbed his eyes. Eyes that had no doubt read a thousand perfectly worded poems over the years. But not tonight.

'Should You Go for a Dump in a Unisex Toilet?'

'No.'

It was possibly the shortest poem ever written. One word. Two letters. But the class seemed to be in full agreement with the sentiment. Even Colin Henson appeared to scrunch his nose up, pull a Robert De Niro style face of nodding agreement and ushered us back to our seats.

'Ok so you still have one final task. A poem about something that's happened recently.

Slightly longer if you can. Longer than one word this time please, Ellie, as lovely as that was.'

'What do you reckon Danny? What you gonna write about? I've pretty much finished mine.'

'I don't know really. I want to make this one a bit more personal maybe. What have you written about?'

'That film you ruined the other week when we were watching Netflix in mine.'

'Ruined?'

'Snakes on a Plane.'

'Yeah, I didn't ruin it, all I said was that...'

Film Ruiner

Snakes on a plane? Simple, you said

Just turn off the heating in the fuselage

It'll send them to sleep

And that shark in Finding Nemo?

The water temperature would kill it

IT'S A FILM!!

CRABS DON'T WEAR HATS!!

STARFISH DON'T BREAKDANCE!!

Can't we just watch it together and enjoy it

That's what I want most

But no, 'The titanic is going to sink, you know?'

'...and Bruce Willis is a ghost'

'A round of applause there for Ellie! Well done, Ellie...I couldn't agree more. Mrs Henson is forever ruining films for me. Return of the Jedi. Said she couldn't watch it after just five minutes because, and these are her words not mine, 'it's just these two metal men walking around a desert. Anyway...Danny...are you ready? You're still scribbling away there.'

'Yeah...erm...just crossing a few bits out. One sec...'

Ellie smiled awkwardly at me and seemed to know what I was writing about. I've never had a very good poker face.

I stood and faced everyone in the poetry class but fixed my gaze on Ellie. And began to feel a bit emotional. And Ellie could see it...and mouthed *'Are you ok?'* at me, which made me feel even more emotional. But wanted. She always knew what to say.

'Erm, this is about something that happened a couple of weeks

91

ago…it's a little bit from the heart but I think this is the best way I can say what I've been wanting to say. It's called Love Letter and it's for Ellie.'

Love Letter

I never meant to shout I never meant to swear

I never meant to look down on you

You're all I want

You're all I need

Nothing more

Please don't look down

You are my A…my B…my C…my D…

My love letter.

This is your poem.

This is my love letter

You're all I want to breathe

Please don't look down

Ellie…as she always would at moments like this…looked down. But then she looked back up. And she smiled a teary smile at me.

That fucking smile.

How had I gone so long in life without seeing that fucking smile.

She walked over to me and I responded by walking towards her even quicker and straight into a deep hug. I whispered

'I'm sorry' again. She nestled her face into my neck and I breathed in deeply.

An inward breath that I would only ever breathe when with her.

Lisa Burnell

Aged 32, and a brief office romance, encapsulated perfectly in one moment when she walked on to my floor as I was sat amongst my team and excitedly handed me a gift. A gift referencing something I told her I was a big fan of. It was hot. It was tasty. And it came in green packaging. And she gave me it right there and then in full view of everyone. As a result, Lisa Burnell was known by one thing by the rest of the team for the next 8 months. Known by the item she had lovingly passed to me that memorable Tuesday afternoon.

'Hey Danny. Are you still seeing Pot Noodle?'

Pot Noodle, sorry, Lisa, was a big fan of kissing. To a certain two songs. And to this day, whenever I hear Sadness or Return to Innocence by Enigma, I will instantly be catapulted back in time to reminisce about Lisa Burnell's intense passion, her ridiculously busy tongue and more, maybe more than anything, I will instantly acknowledge that little brown packet of soy sauce you get with a chicken and mushroom Pot Noodle.

Quiz Night

'Oh God.'

'What is it, Danny? You look like you've seen a ghost.'

'Is that Justin? And Wendy?'

Ellie looked over towards the corner of the pub and let out a little squeal.

'It is!!'

Ellie waved, squealed a little bit louder and caught Wendy's attention who reciprocated the squeal at the exact same pitch. Me and Justin opted for the less squealy male nod of acknowledgement towards each other.

'Ellieeeeee…Dannyyyyy…come and sit here, we can be a team!'

I looked around the half full pub and reluctantly pulled two stools up to the table.

'How did you get here Danny? Where did you park? It was gridlocked up by the bypass, wasn't it? Should've come off at the 32 in hindsight'

Fuck's sake, here we go. Longest night of my life ahead. And he's driving, so not even drinking. This is going to be painful.

'Oh, we got a taxi here, we can have a few drinks plus you never know, if we win the quiz and the bar tab…'

'Well, I'm not sure about my Wendy, her general knowledge isn't up to much but I more than make up for her. I was on my quiz team in school and there's nothing I don't know about formula 1. If there's

any questions on the size of car engines as well, that bar tab is as good as ours. I'll just get a lemonade or something with my share.'

Kill. Me. Now.

Ellie and Wendy were discussing the fact that two or more planets being close together in the zodiac could be harmonious or inharmonious depending on the alignment of something or other I still don't understand.

I turned back to Justin and for the only time in my life, thought I'd rather listen to his stories about Jensen Button, 2.2 litre engines and the quickest route to get to Grantham via the A1.

Thankfully, the quiz was about to start, so I was spared any more of Justin's tripe.

'Right, Ellie...Wendy...we need a team name, quick. They're passing the papers around.'

Without missing a beat, Justin cut in.

'Top Gear.'

Fuck me. Please. Something without cars. Anything.

'What about something about you two loving horoscopes and astrology? Anything?'

Wendy chirped in this time, clearly excited.

'WRITTEN IN THE STARS!!'

'No, that's rubbish Wendy, we need something better than that.'

Justin was already in full pain in the arse mode, wanting to belittle all around him.

'No, I like it', I said. *'Let's go with it.'*

Ellie agreed.

'Yeah, let's go with that. Hey, and if we lose, we might still get a 'constellation' prize.'

Ellie was very proud of her joke. But not as proud as I was. I stood up and gave my own solitary round of applause. Justin sat silently, taking the pen, furiously scribbling 'Written in the Stars' at the top of our quiz sheet.

'Which mythological creature was famously half man half beast?'

It was this moment when I realised Justin was a grifter. One of these people who claim to be knowledgeable but have been faking it for years. I looked at him with one eyebrow raised as he confidently leant over and whispered the answer to the famous mythological creature, famous for being half man, half beast.

'Buffalo Bill. It's Buffalo Bill'

'I don't think it is you know, Justin. He wasn't mythological. I think it's the minotaur.'

He instantly realised he was wrong.

'Yeah, yeah sorry, the minotaur. I always get those two mixed up.'

'You always get Buffalo Bill and the minotaur mixed up?'

'Yeah, well they've both got horns haven't they.'

Fuck me. Quick, give him a question on junctions or service stations. This numpty probably thinks Argos was the Greek god of catalogues.

'Question 7. If you were born between the twenty second of December and the nineteenth of January, what would your star sign be?'

The squeals emanating from Ellie and Wendy's mouths could have been heard for miles.

Dogs from all four corners of the country were tilting their heads, wondering where this high-pitched noise was coming from.

'*CAPRICORN!!!*'

'*Shush,Wendy! People can hear you!!*'

'*Oh, you shush, Justin.You thought the Faroe Islands were in Egypt five minutes ago.*'

Me and Ellie looked at each other and laughed. We'd have liked to have had a night out together, just the two of us, but watching Justin implode like this was too good to miss.

'*And in second place with 29 out of 40….is…Written in the Stars…which means tonight's winners, with an impressive 35 out of 40 and our winners for the 6th week running are the Beyonce Know Alls.Well done lads…you can collect your bar tab as usual, whenever you're ready.*'

The three men known as the Beyonce Know Alls did not look like Beyonce Knowles, Michelle Williams or Kellie Rowlands at all. They had more of an air of substitute science teachers with very visible hygiene issues. Their leader shuffled to the bar, with his jeans falling half way down his arse, revealing a holey, very grubby looking pair of bills, bills, bills.

'*We should have beat them.We got some easy ones wrong there. And there wasn't a single question about cars.*'

Justin was still rankled by our defeat. And his wife, Wendy, wasn't letting up on him.

'*Justin! The picture round??You thought Brad Pitt was Ben Shephard?? And you're meant to know about formula 1?? Since when has Lewis Hamilton looked anything like Nelson Mandela?*'

'It was a bad photocopy.'

'Bad photocopy? We were lucky to get second with you on the team. If Destiny's Child won it, then you're like...you're like Density's Child.'

It was a decent line. The humourless Justin didn't seem to think so, as he knocked back his 4th lemonade of the night and grabbed his and Wendy's coats.

'Come on. Let's go. I'm done with these quizzes.'

Wendy gave Ellie a hug, looked and me, mouthed the word *'sorry'* and put her coat on.

As they left, me and Ellie sat closer, laughed at the previous hour's chaos, touched hands, looked into each other eyes and for once managed to ignore the karaoke that had just started in the opposite corner of the pub.

Ignored it that is, until one of the winning Beyonce Know Alls team got up and sang a surprisingly passable version of Halo. For a man with four stains on his t shirt and jeans that Jim Royle would have been proud of, he grabbed his microphone, closed his eyes and sang soulfully as if he'd been brought up in the back streets of Memphis.

'...Remember those walls I built? Well baby, they're tumbling downnnn'

'That's what people don't realise about Beyonce, Ellie. Great singer...but a terrible bricklayer.'

'Danny. That's nowhere near as good as my constellation joke and you know it.'

'It was a great joke. And I don't think I've ever loved you more.'

'Aww Danny. You love me. I love you too.'

The kiss. Fuck.

Where has that kiss been all my life.

'Have you thought about letter R yet, Ellie?'

'I've been thinking about it since my letter P. It was almost a reiki night but I've had a better idea.'

'Are you going to tell me now or is it a surprise?'

'I'll give you a clue. When was the last time we ate meatballs together?'

Tricia Blackburne

I'm 33 and Tricia Blackburne is slightly older than me. We were set up by a mutual friend, went out for drinks and ended up having what at the time seemed like a one-night stand. Until she messaged me 8 hours later and said 'We can do that again whenever you want, you know?', which, when I opened it, was the best thing I'd read since someone had posted on Facebook 'I've just set off a Chinese lantern in memory of my Grandad and I think I've burnt down next door's shed.'

The relationship didn't blossom much further. Tricia Blackburne's claim to fame was that she'd had a boob reduction on the same day of 9/11.

So, on the fateful day that two magnificent towers were brought crashing down to earth, there was also a terrible act of terrorism.

Re-enact First Date

Me and Tom were sat in our usual seats.

Opposite, one of the pub regulars, Jimmy, who was clearly thirteen sheets to the wind, had stood up and walked slowly towards us, and was about to impart some of his limitless sage wisdom upon us.

This was a man who was convinced Christ had won the pub bonus ball a week earlier, when it was actually someone called Chris T. The man who said someone didn't leave the house for 18 years because they had arachnophobia. The man who complained about the jukebox in the pub just playing 'all of that Ministry of Defence dance shite'

'Alright lads...'

'Alright Jim, how's things?'

'Things are good. Things are always good...I'm more concerned about things for you two youngsters.'

'We're both all good, Jim...no problems here.'

'Yeah, you youngsters never have any worries...never have any concerns but let me tell you both something I learned a long time ago.'

Tom leant in towards me and whispered.

'Here we go...'

'You see lads, every year is like your own book. And your book has got 365 pages. So, you've got to make the most of your story and live every day as if it's your last. As if it's the last time you'll ever

see each other ever again. I've had 71 books. 71.You've got to make your story worthwhile and keep changing it all the time.'

And Jimmy didn't wait for a response. He just walked slowly towards the door and looked over to the bar, where Brenda, who had heard this particular story told dozens of times, looked over, nodded her head and said *'Same time tomorrow, Jimmy?'*

'Same time tomorrow, Bren.'

I looked at Tom, who was pulling the same, quizzical face as I was.

'Not VERY inspiring, is it?'

Ellie had been staying in my flat a lot more. The toothbrush had been in for a while but more and more things were gradually appearing. Her side of the bed was now home to a wax melt burner, a draw full of hair products and was generally a lot more aesthetically pleasing than my side, which had a bottle of two-day old water resting on top of Paulo Coelho's book 'The Pilgrimage', which I'd been making hard work of for a good while, trying to get more and more into my spiritual side.

This time, we headed to Amalia restaurant together. As a proper couple. In a proper relationship.

'I've noticed you know, Ellie.'

'Noticed what?'

'You're wearing the same clothes as the first time we went to Amalia.'

'Danny! I didn't think you would. But thank you!'

'You looked gorgeous.You look gorgeous.'

And she did. Effortless. Summery dress. Doc Martens. Confidence exuding from her…but in a shy way. Manga eyes, like an anime princess…which every so often would show the briefest glimpse of sadness before returning to their natural emerald glow.

We managed to be sat at the same table we had sat at on our first date and I handed Ellie a menu.

'I know what you're thinking Ellie.'

'What am I thinking?'

'You're thinking you want the meatballs again.'

'We're re-enacting the first date, aren't we? Plus, they were GREAT meatballs.'

'Were you nervous on our first date? I was a mess, especially when you first walked in. I fancied you straight away you know.'

'Yeah, I was nervous too. I didn't know what to do or say but a big hug is always a good starting point, right? I don't think I shut up for the entire date…I think that was probably nerves…but I remember liking the fact you were touching my hand and looked interested in whatever nonsense I was spouting. I remember talking a lot about TV chefs.'

'You weren't talking nonsense at all. Same bottle of wine as last time?'

Again, the date was effortlessly comfortable. 20% serious and 80% daftness. Seamlessly drifting from conversations about our jobs, our dreams and our health, before moving into deeper more meaningful territory such as the best way to roast a potato, what film we'd like to see remade but using only Muppets as the actors and if we were to get a tattoo of someone from a Quentin Tarantino film, which one would we get.

'What about spirituality then, Danny? Have you finished The Pilgrimage yet? Or are you making it last, like that bottle of water on top of it?'

'I've almost finished both. There's a lot of talk about re-births, the road of the common people and learning to communicate with the universe…kind of…talking to inanimate objects…animals… insects…it's a hard slog to be honest but I'm getting through it.'

'Well, my Uncle Alex has walked that very walk from start to finish numerous times. And he says it can change your life. You just have to open your mind.'

Ellie sipped the last of her wine as I paid the bill.

'Right, that's all sorted, I'm just nipping to the toilet before we go…'

I helped Ellie put her coat on, watching her giggle as we struggled to get one of her arms in.

'Stop messing Ellie, I'm bursting here!'

'Ok, I'm in… hurry up, I'll wait here.'

As I emerged from the bathroom, I looked over to our table but Ellie wasn't there. I looked out of the window to see her stood on the pavement, with late night traffic flashing past her. I walked towards the door and saw a face I recognised. The same face that had stopped me on our first date. The same face I had seen at the Holistic Health and Wellbeing Day.

'How weird is this! Erm…sorry, I mean, hi! Hey, we're like old friends now!'

'Hi Sagittarius. Did you have the meatballs again?'

'We did! And we still haven't dropped a single one between us.'

'Maybe it's a sign? You're meant to be? Aries…Sagittarius. You're compatible.'

'Because of meatballs?'

I looked outside to try and get Ellie's attention and bring her back in but she was looking in the opposite direction.

'Look, I've got to go…she's outside getting cold…it was nice seeing you again…'

'You too…see you next time…'

'Oh, I don't think I've ever caught your name?'

But by the time I'd asked, she'd turned and walked in the opposite direction.

Lisa Lamb

I went to junior school with Lisa Lamb and ended up dating her for three months around twenty years later after bumping into her in a pub one night and making her laugh.

'You know what, Lisa Lamb, I think you were the only person in our school with an animal for a surname, apart from Joanne Elephant.'

Lisa, it turned out was quite a religious person and maybe as a result, wasn't the most adventurous person in the bedroom. The last I heard, she had travelled to Argentina to help build churches, so a lot of her life still revolved around missionary.

Santiago - El Camino

'So how long has this actually been planned for, Danny?'

Me and Tom were sat nursing our pints of Guinness and picking at a bag of scampi fries which was opened between us on the pub table.

'I told Ellie a couple of months ago when we had a night in hers. And about a week before I almost fucked the whole thing up. I'd been reading Paulo Coelho's book The Pilgrimage and bought her a copy. I finally finished it on Wednesday.'

'It's a religious walk, isn't it? But you're just doing the second half of it, right? And ending up in Santiago? That's your letter S?'

'That's a lot of questions, Tom. Yes, yes, yes and yes.'

'You do know you're not religious though, right?'

'You don't have to be. It's about the experience. And anyway, I've been to church. I was in the Scouts, the Cubs before that and the Beavers before that.'

'Go on, say it.'

'Say what?'

'You've mentioned you were in the Beavers. You always say it. Just say it.'

'Well...now that you've mentioned it, did you know that me and a lady from Leeds called Sharon who appeared in Readers Wives magazine in September 1989 have got something in common?'

Tom sighed.

'No, what have you and a lady from Leeds called Sharon who appeared in ReadersWives magazine in September 1989 got in common?'

'We've both won beaver of the month.'

'Do you feel better now? Good. Jesus, Ellie's got two and a half weeks of this with you. What time do you leave tomorrow?'

'8am. Flight to Bilbao.'

It was going to be the longest time me and Ellie had spent in each other's company 24-7 but we were ready.

'Fail to prepare. Prepare to fail, Ellie. You know who said that? Benjamin Franklin.'

'Have you got your passport, Danny?'

'Oh shit, no, hang on. Tell the Uber driver to wait there. Two minutes.'

I had The Pilgrimage safely packed in my bag, ready to pick up and try and understand it more along the way.

'When you travel, you experience. It's very practical…the act of a re-birth perhaps. Confronting completely new situations and generally not having a clue about the language surrounding you… you're like a child out of the womb again. But still watching. Still taking everything in. Experiencing memories and episodes to remember for the rest of your life. Just remain open minded at all times.'

We have a long, long walk ahead of us. Physically, we're ok. And we're mentally tough. I think.

I knew I'd be spending the next couple of weeks with the right person. It was Ellie's sense of fun that I loved, coupled with the fact that she always fitted in wherever and whatever the location was. Nobody rocked a backpack and walking shoes like Ellie. She looked like a bookish Lara Croft. At any given moment she could either be somersaulting and searching for relics while surrounded by danger or doing an impression of Arnold Rimmer and quoting a line from Red Dwarf. Not to mention the little dimple on the right side of her face which I was always drawn to no matter what she was saying.

'So here we go, Ellie', I said, opening a page of The Pilgrimage which I'd bookmarked.

'According to Paulo Coelho, a religious pilgrimage has always been one of the most objective ways of achieving insight. Always walking forward, adapting yourself to new situations and tackling them head on. Ellie? Are you listening? Come on...what are you taking photos of?'

'You've got to stop and smell the roses, Danny.'

'Oh yeah, I've heard something similar. A galloping horse never smells the roses.'

Ellie looked down very quickly and said *'Yeah, I don't really like that phrase. I think mines a bit more to the point. I prefer that. You've got to stop and smell the roses. You don't have to do this walk in a record time, Danny. That's all. Take your time. Take in your surroundings. Look upwards.'*

I loved that she'd said *'look upwards'*. It was all I wanted from her.

'Stop and smell the roses.' was pretty much Ellie's mantra as we walked day after day. 30 kilometres after 30 kilometres, always arriving into our next destination together.

A 35-kilometre walk. Our feet are already stinging and

wrapped in plasters. There are nuns offering foot massages and dance lessons but we choose to sit in a garden as the sun sets.

Italian teenagers are doing some kind of Brazilian Ju-Jitsu with each other on the garden, near a half empty bottle of red wine. Definitely their own way of flirting. It's the equivalent of me pulling Holly Budgens's hair in Primary School to show her how much I love her.

Maybe I should have just done a flying triangle on her or got her to fall for me via a reverse arm bar.

Religious people are stopping us every so often as we walk mile after mile.

We were handed a piece of paper as we left one American couple and as soon as we'd walked ahead, I unfolded the piece of paper and began to read.

'Blessed are you pilgrim, if you discover that the Camino holds a lot of silence and that a meeting with Our Father is awaiting you. Blessed is the pilgrim if you search and find the One who is the Way, the Truth and the Life'

I looked ahead into the hazy distance, squinted at the sunlight searing through the brilliant yellow fields. I wiped the sweat from my brow, took a longer, deeper than usual gulp of my ice-cold water and whispered to myself and out of Ellie's earshot…

'Seems like a load of nonsense to me…no…hang on. Open mind. Come on, Danny.'

That evening, we found a cosy restaurant and ordered our pilgrim's meals.

'Danny, I think that man is walking over to us.'

'Which man?'

I turned around and a gargantuan behemoth of a human being, who almost filled up the entire small restaurant we were sat in, began to loom over us.

'Are you guys' English? I was listening in a bit but wasn't quite sure!!'

'Hi, yeah, we're English. Danny. This is my girlfriend, Ellie.'

Ellie smiled. She loved it when I introduced her to someone as my girlfriend.

'Brian. Brian Stanton. Stanton carpets.'

Why has he told us where he works? I'm not going to buy a carpet off him. I'm already carrying enough stuff around on my back. A rolled-up rug is going to make things much more difficult.

'Geez I love that you guys are walking this thing. I'd love to do it with my wife but she got kinda sick recently and... well...you know...'

Right Danny. This is the bit where you remember that Brian Stanton from Stanton Carpets has JUST told you his wife has been sick. I know you've had a bottle of wine and a coffee with a third of a bottle of brandy in despite you asking for 'just a drop' but PLEASE get your head on straight and have some fucking self-awareness. You're usually pretty good at that. Just ask a question about carpets. Rugs. Shag pile something or other, for fucks sake.

'So, why she couldn't make the walk then?'

I got a glare off Ellie. It was a GREAT glare. If they were giving out Oscars for the best glare of all time, this was clear favourite and would have probably swept every award. Bafta Glare, Golden Globe Glare. The lot.

'Oh shit…I…er…sorry Brian…I didn't….'

'It's ok man! Look, just because she's not here anymore doesn't mean I have to stop and just see out my life sitting at home. Or in the carpet store. She wouldn't have wanted that. You've gotta keep moving man. Here, let me get us a bottle of wine to share.'

Ellie smiled. She looked up and nodded at the actions and thoughts of a stranger we had only met ten minutes ago.

The Camino spirit in full living glory.

'What about Brian then, Ellie?'

'I love him. I wonder what his wife was like. Quick, he's coming back.'

I shuffled up towards Ellie, Brian returned with a bottle of wine and sat next to me, almost squashing the pair of us in one fell swoop.

'You're pretty cool, you know, Danny. I like your vibe. You're kinda relaxed with people. I wish I was like that.'

'You're pretty cool too, Brian. Me and Ellie think so anyway.'

'Geez man, that's real kind but I'm guaranteed to be THE most uncool man in most places. I remember the night I met Jelena. She was in the club with all of these tanned, cool, beautiful clubbers and they all had these matching red berets on…they were like a professional dance troupe. And I wanted in. I wanted a red beret.'

'So did you get one?'

'They made me dance for one, Danny. Like a big American performing seal. But you know what…they seemed to like my moves and I was given a beret. I was in!'

'Yes! There you go. You were in a dance troupe wearing a red beret! That immediately makes you cooler than me.'

'Danny. I caught sight of myself in the nightclub mirror, man. My glasses were steaming up with the heat inside the club and my hair was going frizzy and sticking out of the sides of the beret. Danny...I looked like Art Garfunkel on ecstasy.'

There is nothing I love more than when someone makes me laugh out loud. Nothing.

Brian Stanton from Brian Stanton carpets then spent the next thirty minutes telling us of a love story that him and his late wife Jelena had written since they were sixteen years old up until...well...you know...

Despite our feet, bones and everything else being sore beyond words, me and Ellie held each other close in bed that night. She nestled underneath my shoulder and moved her nose around for a bit, getting comfy before lifting her head towards me and looking at me directly in the eye.

'Danny...'

'Hi...'

'Can I ask you something?'

'Of course. Anything.'

'What kind of carpet do you think Brian's got in his house?'

I smiled back at her and kissed her on the forehead before she nestled back into my neck.

'Night, Ellie.'

Two shorter days walking. More friendly walkers to chat to.

A Norwegian couple called Ragnar and Aleksandra. two of the healthiest looking people I had ever seen.

'So, whereabouts in Norway do you live?'

'Ah, we live in a beautiful municipality called Fredrikstad.We knew each other from little school.'

'Fredrikstad? Oh right. Ok.'

Don't say it, Danny. Don't say what you're about to say. You know what you're about to say though don't you. So go on. Just say it.

'Is...is that anywhere near Oslo?'

YOU DON'T EVEN KNOW WHERE FUCKING OSLO IS! WHY ARE YOU ASKING THE DISTANCE BETWEEN TWO PLACES IN NORWAY THAT YOU HAVE ZERO KNOWLEDGE OF?'

'It's not too far, Danny. Maybe similar to your Liverpool and Manchester distances, right?'

I nodded sagely and me and Ellie quickly walked on, soon beginning to close the gap on another couple of walkers, one of whom turned to see us approaching.

'Oh hey!!! Buen Camino to you two!! Where y'all from?'

It was Jacob. And his wife, Marsha. Maybe around 70 years old. Faces worn by years of sun. Hardcore walkers by all accounts, judging by the sandals they were wearing.

I walked slightly ahead with Jacob, while Ellie walked with Marsha.

Jacob is an ex-marine and navy seal from Holland. He reminds me of a religious George Carlin. Piercing blue eyes and quite straggly white hair. He's an ex-hippy. So still a hippy, I suppose. He'd met Marsha after giving up alcohol and drugs and now lived a peaceful life in Israel, owning a Kibbutz and helping out people in need.

They met after they'd both found God. I knew it was coming. Within ten minutes he asked if I ever thought of finding God and I told him that the only two people I ever took guidance from are no longer here.

'I lost my folks too, Danny. Sucks don't it. I still talk to them every now and again you know.'

Jacob told me of an interesting past. A life well lived.

'You're an interesting man, Jacob. I think you're an alpha male. Would you say you're an alpha male?

'I'm not really, Dan. Can I call you Dan? Sometimes I'm loud and I tell stories but I'm quiet really. Everyone is quiet deep down. Everyone is the same at night time. Once the lights go off. I was depressed for twenty years. It comes back sometimes but the fresh air helps. And Marsha helps.'

'Ellie helps me, Jacob.'

'She seems great! I've never seen anyone wear a pair of walking boots like she does.'

'Yeah. She really is great. So, have you and Marsha got any children?'

'Yes, we had Mario kind of late in life. He's not really into walking and stuff, doesn't really like sports, doesn't like films, doesn't like music...'

'Wow, there's not much left. Is he a gamer?'

'Is he gay?'

'Noooo! Is he a gamer! You know like X-Box?'

'Haha oh right a gamer. I see.Yeah, I guess he used to play on those sometimes.'

Me and Jacob started laughing and I improvised a little sketch of how that coming out scene went.

'Erm. Mom. Dad. Can we have a talk, I've got something I need to tell you.'

'Sure, son. Anything.You know me and your mom have always been here for you.'

'Well. I…er…I've been out today and… I …I bought a PlayStation.'

'Hey. No matter what you do Mario, we'll always be proud of you. And your brother. Luigi.'

Jacob was laughing.

'You know, I'd been feeling kinda blue today, Dan… it's been nice talking to you.You're funny. But you don't wear those boots as well as Ellie.'

Me and Ellie slept well that evening. We knew we had three days walking through La Meseta, seventy-two hours across what I had read and had been told was an arid, breathless stretch of desert. A long, flat section of the walk, known amongst pilgrims for its wide skies, dry heat and flat lands, all of which have been known to distort perceptions of time and distance.

My alarm went off as usual at 6:45am.

'Hey.'

Ellie leant in to me and kissed my cheek.

'Hey.You're up. How long have you been awake?'

'I woke up at 5:55.'

'Again?'

'Again. My angel numbers.'

'What does this one mean again?'

'It symbolises spiritual guidance and learning. It's associated with transition, freedom and helps you manifest your ideal life.'

'I think that's what I need. I might set my alarm for 5:55 tomorrow.'

'NO!! That doesn't count. It's got to happen naturally. Come on, Danny. Get up and stretch.You were walking like Forrest Gump in his callipers for the first twenty minutes yesterday.'

We headed out onto the streets with our dusty backpacks on our aching backs and spotted Jacob and Martha already sat at a table, drinking a coffee and eating a pastry.

'Dan! Ellie! You decided to have a lie in then!'

'Morning Jacob…hi Martha…'

'Pastry?', he offered, pointing one towards us.

'No thanks, we've packed a few bits, we'll probably get going… don't want to be walking at the height of the sun later on.'

'Don't forget to eat, Dan. Energy, remember? Here, we've also got some chips, take a chip, please.'

'There's quite a lot of mayonnaise on those, Jacob.'

Jacob looked at me as if he was about to scold me.

'Dan. Chips without mayonnaise is not chips. Oh, and also…for you some more advice.'

'Sure.What's that? Is it about mayonnaise again?'

'No, Dan.Wear sunscreen. If I could offer you only one tip for the *future, sunscreen would be it.'*

'Wait. That's Baz Luhrmann, right? Don't worry about the future. Or, worry but know that worrying is as effective as trying to solve an algebra equation by chewing bubble gum.'

'That's it, Dan! Do something every day that scares you. Don't be reckless with other people's hearts. And don't put up with people who are reckless with yours.'

Martha looked at Jacob and added her own line from the song.

'Keep your old love letters and throw away your old bank statements.'

Jacob smiled back at Martha and kissed her on her lips. I'd have loved to have seen photographs showing their own love story through the years. I imagined them to be stunning looking and beyond cool when in their twenties and thirties and beyond.

I led Ellie on the Camino way and we started the days first few steps hand in hand, feeling good about the day ahead.

As we walked away, Jacob shouted one last time. *'Dan!! Your hat!! Mad dogs and Englishmen!! OH…AND TRUST ME ON THE SUNSCREEN!'*

He laughed to himself as Martha stared back at him and shook her head.

We had only been walking for a couple of hours and Ellie was beginning to slow down.

'It's these blisters Danny. I'm ok…I can walk but I'm struggling.'

'Here. Sit here. Let me have a look. We've got loads of first aid. Those plasters are coming off, they're rubbish. Here, I'll put a

couple of these on.'

'Aww you're protecting me. I love when you look after me, Danny. With your little pencil case full of plasters. And your whistle.'

'It's not a pencil case; it's my first aid box. Look, this one's bleeding. Sit still. Stop messing about. Don't look down at your feet it'll hurt more.'

We carried on walking, slower than usual as the sun started to beat down upon us.

'I don't think I can walk tomorrow. I need a day off, Danny.'

'Let me see your foot. Jesus Christ. Erm. I mean it doesn't look that bad.'

'Not that bad? Danny, you could fit a Malteser in that hole. Those plasters aren't worth a carrot. Look, I don't want you to stop walking. I can get one of those cars that take people's luggage to the next stop. Brian Stanton does it every day.'

'Brian Stanton?'

'Yes, Brian Stanton. Brian Stanton from Brian Stanton carpets, remember? You thought his wife was alive forty-five seconds after he'd told you she wasn't alive?'

'Oh shit, yeah. Brian Stanton from Brian Stanton carpets. No chance. We're walking together or not at all.'

'Danny. Look at me. Just walk. I'll be waiting for you. I need one day off that's all.'

So that's what we did.

The following day and for the first time on the Camino, I felt alone. My immediate surroundings were bleak. The odd tree. Rocks. Endless, endless dusty roads. I'd been walking alone for three hours and had barely seen a soul, with another three hours walking still ahead of me.

I knew Ellie was safe and I wasn't anxious...definitely not frightened. Not like I was when I was a child and had that horrific memory of losing my Mum in the supermarket for three seconds which seemed like an eternity.

I was alone on this path and even if I was to scream, no one could hear me. Yet I thought about doing it anyway.

Just for a release.

Another hour passed. I still hadn't seen a soul.

Another hour.

I looked over to my right side as a flash of colour flew into my eyeline.

And then to my left side as another flash of colour flew into my eyeline.

Two burnt orange butterflies had appeared either side of me.

'What do you two want?'

And there we had it. Madness had set in. I was talking to butterflies.

'Come on. What do you two want? I haven't got anything for you, sorry. Go away. Go on.'

I walked ahead.

And the two burnt orange butterflies followed me.

Either side of me.

Not moving like a butterfly would normally move though, aimlessly floating in all directions.

They were fluttering straight along and right by my sides.

'Ok you two. Listen up. Maybe I'm going fucking crazy here. You. Stay there for a second. Have you got a little grey moustache? Are you about to bollock me for leaving a fridge door open? And you... how come you left me in the supermarket for three seconds when I was five years old? If you're really who I think you are, ask me how the away goals rule in football works, then fly away, come back again and then ask me the same question over and over again.'

The two burnt orange butterflies stayed alongside me for another minute or so before floating off together.

Which is when it happened.

A kind of energy and release which I can only describe as being like a thousand shivers down my spine left my body and I kneeled down on to the dusty road.

I felt like crying but I couldn't.

I felt like screaming but I couldn't.

I felt like swallowing. But I couldn't.

And I thought of Ellie. And I saw a silhouette.

Fucking hell, she looks even more beautiful in a mirage. She began to speak, softly and dreamlike.

'I told you Danny. I told you it was true. I told you about butterflies, remember? No... you weren't listening. Listen now. It's about transformation and your soul's journey. The metamorphic process from caterpillar to butterfly is your re-birth. You're breaking free from the darkness.'

And as quickly as she had appeared, she began to disappear. Only to be replaced by a much larger silhouette.

'Get out, Tom. I don't need your logic now. ELLIE! COME BACK!!'

Tom's silhouette outline began to speak slightly more purposefully.

'I told you Danny. I told you all of this is nonsense. You see, what's happened here is those two burnt orange butterflies have seen a big sweaty oaf. That's you. A lump. And you're a lumpy oaf who's full of moisture and you smell terribly and they're interested in you. It's as simple as that. Or maybe, it could be something to do with the anechoic chamber, whereby purely because you've spent so much time alone, in this heat, isolated, your senses are naturally...'

'THERE'S ELLIE AGAIN. GET OUT, TOM!!'

She's even clearer now. Not just a silhouette. A stunning mirage.

'Danny. I think they were there with you. You've carried your photograph of them since we started walking. I think they were with you. Like they always were and always will be. They're with you.'

And the beautiful feeling of a thousand shivers down my spine stopped just as suddenly as it had started and I found myself alone, in the deserted plains, still dropped to my knees.

I looked around, hoping to see the two burnt orange butterflies but they had long gone. I just wanted them both back.

To say thank you.

And to tell them I would see them again but I had to leave to meet Ellie and that they'd love her. She made me happy. She worked hard. She was strong. She was beautiful. She held doors open for people.

And then I stood. And I smiled.

And I felt at peace.

And I thought maybe life's journey isn't about becoming anything. Maybe it's about unbecoming everything that isn't really you, so that you can be who you were meant to be in the first place.

I raced to the next village, where Ellie was waiting for me.

She hopped towards me, arms outstretched and this time, I put my head down into her shoulder.

'How was the walk? You're pretty much the first one here. Did you run?'

I just looked at Ellie and she looked back at me.

'What is it? What happened Danny?'

So, I explained what had happened on La Meseta, not fully knowing if what had happened had actually happened. I spoke for maybe ten minutes. Uninterrupted.

Ellie sat. Listened. Smiled. Nodded. Smiled again. I was physically and mentally exhausted.

The next morning, I woke before my 6:45am alarm.

I picked up my phone and stared at the time for what seemed like an eternity.

And just as the numbers on my phone screen flicked to 5:56am, I looked over at Ellie, who was still fast asleep.

Tarot Reading

'You know, I'm still really sorry about Santiago, Danny. I really wanted to finish the walk. I wanted to go to our letter S. I messed it up for us. I'm so mad with myself.'

'You haven't messed up at all. Look, we'll go back again one day, I promise.We'll do the whole thing from start to finish.We tried to walk too far too soon. Maybe I should have picked Skegness after all.You could have won another blue, two-foot dragon at the fair.We could have got on another broken ghost train.'

Ellie gave me a half smile but I knew deep down she wanted to walk all the way to Santiago.

She felt as though she'd let us both down but there was no way a person could walk long distances with their feet, as dainty as they are, looking like two chewed and spat out Pickled Onion Monster Munch.

But my excitement for Ellie's next date choice had been ramped up after my experience on La Meseta. I was starting to see the world differently and had a new calmness, frequently being transported back to seeing the two burnt orange butterflies and the feeling of a thousand shivers down my spine.

I no longer feared anything. Especially death.

I'd watched both parents die in front of my eyes and I was beginning to feel a total inner peace as the world around me continued to lose its shit at the most absurd, pointless nonsense.

Your laptop is frozen?

So what?

The train was three minutes late?

So what?

Your doctor's receptionist was short with you?

So what?

None of it meant anything. The more the chaos surrounding me increased the calmer I became.

Someone raised their voice at me?

The calmer I became.

Someone pushed past me?

The calmer I became.

Someone didn't hold a door open for me?

The calmer I became.

It didn't matter.

One thousand shivers down my spine.

One thousand shivers down my spine.

It was the only feeling I craved.

'We'll go back and walk the whole thing again, Ellie. I swear. Come on. Here. One milky tea. That'll perk you up. And we've both got something to look forward to this weekend. The Tarot reading.'

'Are you really looking forward to it, Danny? You're not just saying it?

'You know, since what happened in Santiago, I've opened up my mind and my eyes to it even more. Don't tell Tom but maybe this

Tarot reading might even influence my future. Our future?'

'Dannyyyyyyyyyyy!!'

She was using a lot of y's again. Always a sign of Ellie's excitement. The more letter y's on the end of my name, the more excited she became.

'You're really looking forward to it? I love you! You know, I thought about starting my own Tarot reading business once?'

'You should still do it. Do something every day that scares you. Say yes more.'

'I had a name and everything. Gemma Stone.'

'Gemma Stone? Wait. Gemma. Stone. Gemstone?'

'Why are you looking at me like that, Danny?'

'Like what?'

'Like you're about to burst out laughing. You're doing that little thing with your mouth. You're biting your lip. Stop laughing at me!'

'I'm not! It's just you know…Gemma Stone…it's a bit too nail on the head, isn't it? Why not Clair Voyant? Krystal Ball? Nominative determinism at its finest.'

'You'll get a nail in the head if you carry on laughing at me.'

I was booked in for a 2pm Tarot reading.

Ellie was booked in for a 2pm Tarot reading.

We looked up and saw the name of the building.

'Here we go. This is it. 'Within The Shadows.'

We'd decided to go into different rooms, with different readers but at the same time.

I had no idea what to expect but, in my mind, I was about to be sat opposite a crazy looking woman with wild eyes and her arms and fingers covered in rings and brightly coloured bracelets. I couldn't have been more wrong as I slowly peered and then walked through a black curtain.

'Hello Danny, I'm Simon.'

Simon was a short, unassuming ginger haired man with a soft southern accent. A crooked smile. An orange football shirt accentuated his freckly arms. Not what I expected at all.

'Sorry I'm a bit out of sorts here, I forgot you were my two o'clock reading. My diary had you down for tomorrow. I've got my cards here in my bag, one sec. I was convinced it was tomorrow. I'm normally right on top of things but I've had so much on my mind lately.'

It didn't fill me with confidence. I looked around Simon's small desk. Everything was perfectly straight and lined up alongside each other. A box full of different coloured stones, various crystals, numerous leaflets about spirituality. The entire room didn't have a thing out of place or at an angle.

'Right then, Danny. So, this is your first time getting a reading?'

'Yes.'

'And you're getting a six-month reading?'

'Yes.'

'Ok. No time like the present then. What I want you do is take a long deep breath in for the count of four and then out again. And do that again three times. Oh, and before you start, I'll need you to uncross your arms. That's it. And your legs as well. We need the

energy to flow as you're breathing. That's it. Good. Now look up to the sky and be calm.'

Why am I panicking? I know how to breath. I know how to uncross my arms. Just relax, Danny. Stop being so nervous. You're shaking. Stop apologising.

'Ok so I want you to pick one from these three piles of cards. This one? Ok...now I'm going to split this into three piles if you can pick one. This one? Ok. Now finally, one last cut and I want you to pick one of these two.'

Jesus Christ, it was like being sat with a ginger David Blaine. Just relax. Deep breaths and uncrossed arms.

'Right, so this is your pile, Danny. I'm going to turn three cards over first and we'll see what you've got.'

Simon proceeded to turn over three cards.

'The Ace of Swords. The King of Swords. The Page of Pentacles.'

I looked at Simon with my eyebrows raised inquisitively, wondering what lay in store.

Swords sounds quite overly aggressive and I have no idea what a Pentacle is. Is it something do with a pen and a tentacle? No of course not. Shut up, Danny. Relax. You're still shaking. Breath. Twice in through the nose and one long one out of the mouth.

Simon looked down at the cards, carefully scanning what was laid in front of us. He stroked his chin and rubbed his hand over his mouth before looking up at me and raising his own eyebrows even higher than I had raised my own.

'Wow. Interesting Danny. Hmmm ok. Let's take a look from the start then...the first card. The Ace of Swords. So, this card is saying to me that you've been seeking or you're going to seek clarity in all

aspects of your life. The Ace of Swords suggests that any challenges you have been facing in your relationships will soon get resolved. It indicates that you might have recently achieved a breakthrough and discovered the truth about your situation. You've found a way of understanding things more clearly and have got the presence of mind to articulate your position a lot better.'

Ok, so that all rang true. Despite hearing a tiny version of Tom on my shoulder, whispering in my ear *'Erm...Danny. It's all a load of bollocks, you know. He could be saying this about any of the cards. Take no notice.'*

But I was taking notice.

Seeking clarity. Tick.

Failed relationships. Tick.
Recent breakthrough. Tick.

Simon continued talking. Calmly and clearly, while looking down at the cards.

'The King of Swords stands for a wise, self-assured and powerful individual who controls their own destiny and the results of their choices. You had something trapped inside you and it just needed to be unlocked. You're in control of your own destiny. You have a clarity and a calmness in your mind and your dreams and desires are going to become a success.'

I'd never classed myself as self-assured, powerful or in control of my own destiny. But now I was starting to see it. To feel it.

'Now ok...this last card. The Page of Pentacles. The Page of Pentacles is advising there are many chances to find love. All that's needed for you is to seize them. Don't hesitate. Take a leap of faith.'

It all rang true. I sat opposite Simon and stared back at him.

He knew that I believed the words he was saying. It was written all over my face. I couldn't lie. Again, I struggled to talk for a moment. Struggled to swallow.

'So, what do you think Danny. Does any of that ring true? Do you have any questions you'd like to ask?

I think Simon was wanting a question along the lines of the reading. A question about clarity in my life. A question about a recent breakthrough. A question about seizing love.

All I could think was *'How am I going to remember all of this for Ellie?'*, so I asked a logical question instead.

'Can I take a photograph of the cards please?'

'Of course! Here, let me turn them around for you. So, the Page of Pentacles hasn't come out for a while. You've got to seize love if you ever find it, Danny.'

'I think I might have already seized it. I'm not sure. She's in the next room. Hey, what happens if she's pulled the Page of Pentacles as well?'

Simon laughed and began to tidy the crystals on his desk, before straightening up the pile of leaflets and handing me a box of stones.

'It could happen. If she picks the Page of Pentacles and both of you need to seize love, then I suppose it'll double your chances. There's a song by James. 'You've got to keep faith that your path will change, you've got to keep faith that your love will change, tomorrow...'

'I know the song. I love the song. So, you'll also know the line 'and we're both scared?'

'There's no need to be, Danny. Here, pick one of these. Yours to keep.'

I looked into the box and moved numerous coloured stones around with my forefinger before settling on one. I could already see the anxiety in Simon's face as I mixed up stones he'd no doubt set out previously in a meticulous, uniform fashion.

'I'll take that one.'

'This one? Good choice. There's a nice little pattern on there. It looks a bit like a white feather.'

I smiled, placed the stone in my wallet, pulled aside the black curtain and went to wait for Ellie.

Ellie closed the door behind her and I may not have ever seen a more excited human being in my life.

'Dannyyyyyyyyyyyyyyyyyyyyyyyyyyyyyy!!!'

I think she'd just set a new record for the amount of letter 'y's in my name.

'I got the Page of Pentacles AND the major cards for justice and LOVE!'

'No way! I got the Page of Pentacles as well. I think. Hang on. Let me look at my phone. Yeah, there it is. The Page of Pentacles. Wasn't it about seizing love?'

'It is!!'

'So, what do the major cards mean? Are they better? More important?'

Ellie was like a woman possessed, her speech like a machine gun, firing out word after word without coming up for breath.

'So, the love card is all about our coming together and our new beginnings and a union of two souls it's two people who are meant

to be together because of their strong emotional and physical connection and it's us, Danny, IT'S US and I got the Justice major card too and she mentioned something about us signing contracts together!!'

'What like...house contracts?'

'Erm...maybe...it could be any kind of contract, I think. A contract between us?'

And we looked at each other and without saying a word, we both knew what we were thinking. But we didn't say anything. We just gave each other the slightest smile.

It was the look you have with your very best friend. Whoever that person may be. Whether it be a male or a female best friend.

That feeling, that look when you can instantly tell what the other person is thinking. You know you've found the one. You want to be with them all of the time and you want to share your life with them. The last person you want to see at night and the first person you want to see in the morning. True love.

That's your soul mate. Right there.

Under the Stars

'I think you're going to like my letter U idea, Ellie. I've been thinking about it ever since you told the greatest constellation joke ever told at the quiz night.'

'Ooh! Ooh! Ooh!'

'You ok there, Bubbles?'

'Ooh! Ooh! Is it what I think it is?'

'I don't know. What do you think it is?'

'Something to do with horoscopes? Stars?

'Well, I suppose it does include stars.'

'Tell me! Come on, spill!'

'Well, the stars could be Ethan Hawke and Julie Delpy.'

'Jesse and Celine! What's this one called? Before Midnight? So, hang on…what's the letter U? I still don't get it.'

'Under the stars. How about this Saturday night? I'm going to set up the TV in the garden, the sofa is going outside, I've got some heaters AND blankets. And we're going to watch the final film and try our best not to set fire to everything and burn down the house.'

Ellie moved in close and put her hands tightly around my waist. She slowly looked up into my eyes and said the words I knew she was going to say and the words that I'd hoped she would say.

'Danny…'

'Yeah?'

'...what sweets shall we get?'

It's not fair, sometimes. Life isn't fair sometimes. It's taken me 38 years to meet this person.

'So, what did you think, Celine?'

'Will we be like that in the future?'

'You mean will we have twins and argue a lot?'

Ellie shrugged her shoulders.

'I mean, hopefully some of it will come true?'

She looked at me in a way she hadn't often looked at me previously. A seriousness. A look suggesting serious commitment mixed with an inquisitiveness, trying in turn to read the level of seriousness and commitment in my own eyes.

'Danny. If we were meeting for the for the first time today, would you take me on another date?'

'Wait, are you doing your movie quote thing? I don't know my lines. Is that even a line?'

'No, It's not from the film. I'm asking you a question. A serious question. Would you take me on another date? Would you say something nice to me? Sometimes I think back to the night you shouted at me and I worry...I worry you might do it again. I don't know why you talked to me like that if you said you loved me.'

Fuck. Think. Don't fuck up this time. Just say how you feel.

'Ellie. Listen, look at me...the nervous Sagittarius you met in Amalia on our first date? That's me. That's who I am. That's the real me and I'll always regret shouting at you. I don't want to hurt you. I never wanted to hurt you.'

She knew I was telling the truth. And not just because I'd fucking said the word Sagittarius. But now I was starting to believe...I think I was starting to believe? For fuck's sake I don't know what to believe.

'Danny, I think I know which movie quote I want us to act. For you to act. It's only one line.'

Ellie tapped into her phone, looked at me and handed it over. I looked at the phone and began to read.

'If you want love, then this is it. This is real life. It's not perfect but it's real.'

And it was real. But to me it was perfect. She was perfect. And more than anything, I wanted her to know it.

'Ellie. I think we'll have some days together that are beautiful and we'll have some days that are incredibly difficult. But you have to remember when things do get difficult, this is the true version of me. The one that loves you more than you know.'

'That's not from the film, is it, Danny?'

I looked into her eyes and I shook my head.

Hannah Brown

I'm 35 years old. Hannah Brown is 35 years old. I have never been married. Hannah Brown has been married. Hannah Brown is now divorced. Me and Hannah Brown are sitting talking in her house one evening and she complains that she never had sex on her wedding night. Hannah Brown says she still has her wedding dress upstairs. Me and Hannah Brown give each other a look which can only mean one thing. Ten minutes later, I am completely naked with a fully wedding dressed Hannah Brown on top of me and I am wondering if I have just been groomed.

Venice

'Venice? Ellie's taking you to Venice??'

'That's right, Tom. Ellie is taking me to Venice.'

'Oh God'

'Oh God, what?'

'You always get nervous in Italy. You've watched Goodfellas and The Sopranos too many times. Not everyone wants to try and kill you, you know. Venice, though, Danny. Wow. And it's not even Valentine's Day.'

'It doesn't have to be Valentine's Day to do something romantic, Tom. What did your Tony say once? 'It doesn't have to be pancake day to enjoy a pancake.'

'Yeah, but our Tony's single now. His wife left him. He was addicted to pancakes.'

As intimidating as I found Italy, surely, I can't fuck this one up.

I was going to one of the world's most picturesque, romantic cities.

With the woman I'm sure is the one. Mine and Ellie's tarot readings called it. She's the one I want to 'sign the contract' with, as unromantic as that sounds.

After 21 dates. 21 letters of the alphabet. Only 5 letters left.

'Why are you panicking, Danny? You look like you've seen a ghost. Wait! Justin hasn't walked in, has he?'

'I'm...I'm ok...I just get a bit nervous in these Italian restaurants. These waiters look terrifying. That one keeps staring at me.'

'He works here. He is supposed to be looking at you. Just relax, capisce?'

'DON'T SAY CAPISCE! Shit, he's coming over. He's heard you say capisce.'

'He's coming over, Danny...because he's going to take our orders. Relax. I'll order for us.'

If anything, the bottle of red wine didn't help with my relaxation. Am I having a panic attack? Look around you, Danny. Look at the restaurant. It's perfect for a date. Look across the table at who is sitting opposite you. She's perfect. Fitting in as always. Elegance and beauty. No one has worn a red dress like that and looked so gorgeous since Chris De Burgh banged on about his ex-wife constantly having to fend off strangers asking her to 'darnce.'

You love her. Tell her you love her.

Whatever you do, don't say something fucking stupid like...

'Quite nice in here isn't it. Don't worry though, Ellie. I wouldn't ask you to marry me in here.'

Ellie looked at me, kind of bemused. Silence.

I'd already spent twenty minutes worrying I was going to be on the receiving end of a mafia hit and now I'd told the person I'd fallen massively in love with that I wouldn't bother proposing to her in one of the most beautiful, perfect settings we'd ever been in.

Silence. Silence. Silence.

The most awkward date of our relationship followed, as I went from bad to worse, forgetting to use my fork and picking up chips with my fingers like a hippopotamus scooping up mud, before attempting to dismantle my lobster like a four-year old child let loose with a pneumatic drill. And what kind of fucking idiot orders chips with lobster, Danny?!

Chris De Burgh never added a verse to describe his own particular Lady in Red having to wipe lobster claw off her dress, which had shot across a table and squirted onto her lap.

Silence. Silence. Silence.

And then home to the hotel, wondering why the fuck I'm allowed to interact with other human beings.

4:44am. I've shot bolt upright and Ellie is at the end of the bed. Fuck. Is she about to hobble me like Kathy Bates in Misery? I only fired an entire lobster claw across the table at her. It's not like I've just killed off the main character in her favourite book.

'It's just the air conditioning, Danny. It's too hot in here.'

'Oh. Ok. You…you coming back to bed?'

Ellie slid in behind me, linked her arms around the front of my stomach and tightly spooned into me. She hugged even tighter, one of the greatest, most intimate feelings in the world, and a wave of relief passed through my entire body.

Ellie leant in, placed her mouth over my ear and whispered *'Just relax over here, Danny. We've still got two days left…let's start afresh tomorrow, capisce?'*

Every time. She knew what to say. Every. Time.

The following day, we wandered aimlessly around the streets of Venice.

'Isn't this meant to be one of the fashion capitals of the world, Ellie?'

'Yeah. So people say.Why?'

'Look at him over there. Cycling shorts? I know it's warm, but... aren't they a little bit too revealing...too tight? He looks like pre packed goose meat.'

Ellie looked over at the offending Lycra.

'Wow.Yeah, that's a bit much. He's not even...filling them...if you know what I mean?'

'Yeah, I know what you mean.'

'It has reminded me of something though.'

'What's that?'

'We need to pick up some button mushrooms when we get home.'

I've said it once and I'll say it again. Make me laugh out loud and I will love you forever.

'Dannyyy! Art museum!'

'Come on let's go in...we can pretend it's our first date and we're doing letter A.'

'Deal!'

I kissed Ellie on the lips and smiled at her.

'Little bit forward for a first date, Danny?'

'Yeah, sorry about that but I'm afraid I'm a Sagittarian and I like to perform the complex dance of flirtation with potential partners.'

Ellie grabbed my arm before racing into the museum, waving to an old Italian gentleman sat at a desk and saying *'Bonasera, Signore!'*

'Bonasera!', he replied, before looking at me, nodding towards Ellie and saying *'Bellissima!'*

I didn't know the Italian for *'You can't take her anywhere'*, so I just panicked and shuffled past him.

As I sat in the museum, I remembered waking up earlier that morning at 4:44. I picked up my phone and tapped *'Angel numbers 444'* into Google.

'This symbolises a powerful message of love, support and guidance from your angels. A reminder you are on the right path and your angels are offering their unwavering support. The number 4 symbolises stability, security and a strong foundation.'

I looked over at Ellie, who was stood in front of a painting.

'Danny! Butterflies!'

Stability. Security.

A strong foundation.

She's the one. I'm convinced.

So, I wrote her a letter, to be opened in the airport on the way home.

I even wrote on the front of the envelope *'To be opened in the airport on the way home.'*

'Ellie.

I'm sorry for the restaurant. I'm a dick. I get tongue tied sometimes. As soon as I saw you in the restaurant, I wanted to kiss you, pick you up and spin you around. Instead, I fired lobster claw across the table at you. I never want to stop spinning you around. I never want to flick lobster at you again. I love you. And I love all the little things about you. I love your impression of Christopher Walken. I love that you said you couldn't wear that meat dress Lady Gaga wore because it'd get all maggoty around the hem. I love you when you're reading poems. I love your tiny feet, even when they've got massive holes in them. I love that you get excited by photographs of animals dressed in human clothes. I love the way that you don't deliberately yawn when I'm telling you a story and you stifle the yawn and pull a weird face even though you know I can see you're stifling a yawn. I love you even though you call my wallet a purse. I love the way you always know what to say. I love the way you never spill meatballs. I love that little bit of your face. I love your brain. I love your kiss. And I love waking up next to you. Capisce? xx'

Wine tasting

'Look, I just wanted it to be me and you, Ellie…that's all.'

'I know but Wendy's saying Justin never takes her out any more and I mentioned the wine tasting this weekend, so…I'm just trying to help a friend that's all.'

'So, I've got three days to learn everything there is to know about Jeremy Clarkson and that other one who crashes vehicles for a living?'

'Danny. Be nice.'

Despite being my choice, I was already hesitant about our letter W date. For a start, the most tedious man on planet earth was going to be there and secondly, I was going to have to pretend to know about wine by *'smelling the bouquet'*, before quaffing what I was supposed to describe as being *'fruity, with a stubborn hint of danger'*, which sounds more like someone describing a Radio 1 DJ.

Then, I'd have to spit, therefore waste, expensive wine clumsily into a silver bucket, already swimming with the scarlet sputum of other so-called experts.

Justin was already tucking into his second glass of wine.

'Glad I left the old soft top at home today, Danny. Don't like leaving her sitting on the driveway though. I'd much rather be showing her off around the village.'

God. He refers to his car as 'her'. Would anyone notice if I coughed blood into one of these silver buckets? There's already some Merlot in that one. I'm sure no-one would be able to tell the difference.

'Well, I'm glad you're having a couple of drinks today, Justin… you seemed a bit pent up at that quiz night we went to? A little bit angry?'

'Rubbish night. Rubbish quiz. And you're still doing this stupid alphabet thing as well aren't you? Well at least that'll be finished soon and you can both start acting like normal people doing normal things…going on normal dates.'

Prick. Absolute prick.

'The only important alphabet, Danny, is the phonetic alphabet. I bet you don't even know it, do you? All us drivers know it. We have to know it.'

Here we go. What a Charlie Uniform November Tango.

'Well, I know what the letter A is, Justin. A is for Alpha.'

'Yes, Alpha. Like me, Danny. An alpha male. Nice car, nice job, nice big garden.'

'I'm sure Wendy and your kids love all that as well.'

'Who?'

'You know. Your wife. She wasn't listed in your top three things just then. Or your kids.'

'Oh her. Wendy. Yeah. She's ok. Ticks a box. Lost a bit of weight recently but wears black a lot to make herself look slimmer. Underneath all that she can still look like a Boxing Day balloon. And the kids? The kids are ok, too. Little pains in the arse most of the time to be honest. So, what others do you know, Danny? Come on.'

'What other what?'

'Letters of the phonetic alphabet, duh!'

Justin had finished his second glass of wine just as quickly as he'd finished his first and was already starting to slur. So, I decided to have some fun.

'Ask me one, then, Justin.'

'B.'

'I don't know.'

'Bravo.'

'Did I get it right?'

'What? No.'

'But you said Bravo.'

'No, you said you didn't know.'

'Oh. Ok. Ask me another.'

'P.'

'Don't know.'

'You don't know P? It's EASY.'

'Give me a clue.'

'A clue? Erm…a clue. Let's see. Ok, I'm one.'

'Prick?'

'What?'

'Prick. You're a prick, Justin.'

'Papa. It's Papa, I'm a father. It's what Benji used to call m..wait… what do you mean I'm a prick?'

'It can only mean one thing, Justin. You. Are. A. Prick. I can't carry on with his anymore, sorry. I didn't even want you to come on this

wine tasting thing if I'm honest. Wendy's great but you've been here twenty minutes and you're already spoiling it. Look over there, Wendy hasn't spoken to you once since we got here and I don't blame her. You're just not nice to be around...little snide quips... little digs at people. I'm done with you.'

I walked over to Ellie and Wendy, who were both giggling, chatting and swilling their large wine glasses around before sticking their noses as far as possible into the glass.

Ellie was already enjoying herself and messing around.

'Well, Wend, I don't know about you but I'm getting a hint of giraffe and lemon sherbets with this cheeky little number. I hope Danny doesn't have too many glasses this afternoon because I wouldn't mind maybe sharing a semillon with him later this evening.'

Despite my hackles being raised after the incident with Justin, I still couldn't help enjoying looking at Ellie enjoying herself and being natural and comfortable with her close friend. But the mood had changed. My mood had changed.

'Come on Ellie...I've got a bit of a headache...I'm not feeling too good. Sorry, Wendy...I'm going to have to go.'

Ellie passed me my jacket and shrugged her shoulders at Wendy, apologetically.

'Bang goes my chance of a semillon, then.'

So that was me and Justin over and done with. At letter W.

And I know what I'd have gone with if he'd have asked me the phonetic alphabet word for that one.

Xtreme Sports

Midnight.

Me and Ellie are lying in bed in each other's arms. The only sound is the sound of our own breathing until she looks at me and begins to speak.

'It's nearly done, Danny. We're at letter X. Three more alphabet dates and then it's done.'

'Maybe we could start over at A again?'

'Maybe. I'm sure you'll think of something else instead. You're good with things like that.'

'So...do you know your X?'

'Can we not talk about my X while we're in bed. We've had such a nice night.'

'Stop messing. Come on.'

'Well, I thought maybe an X-Box night but neither of us like computer games. I was thinking xylophone lessons but neither of us are insane. And I thought about an X marks the spot treasure hunt day but then I remembered...'

'Remembered what?'

'Remember when we went to the lake? When we were driving away from the hideaway?'

And Ellie began to sing softly into my ear.

'Let this night invade my lungs, you're all want to breathe... Right beside the lake, I burnt for you, you burnt for me.'

I smiled.

'The...X-treme sports place?'

'Yeah. The X-treme sports place...I'm going to book it this week for us. We can stay in the hideaway again.'

I looked back into Ellie's eyes and softly continued the song.

'...so, kiss me the way that you would, if we died tonight. And hold me the way that you would, for the final time...

Ellie kissed me softly on the lips before taking over the song again.

'Whatever may come somewhere deep inside, there's always this version of you and I...so kiss me the way that you would, if we died tonight...'

I placed the palm of my hand on the back of her neck and pulled her in even closer.

And I kissed her.

The way that I would if we died tonight.

'Right then you two...have you ever done wakeboarding before?'

Jerry, our wakeboarding instructor had met us at 10am and was already donning a wetsuit that left little to the imagination. He looked like a fifty-year-old Richmond's pork sausage wrapped in red rubber.

'I have!' said Ellie, excitedly putting her hand up. 'Danny hasn't but he loves the water. He's seen Jaws three times as well. Even though it still terrifies him.'

'You're not helping, Ellie. No, I haven't wake boarded before, Jerry. I thought we'd do this first to ease ourselves in. We've got a hang-

gliding lesson at two o'clock this afternoon as well, provided we're still alive.'

'Hang gliding! You'll be fine. Phil will look after you, he's been teaching that longer than I've been doing this and I've been doing this for 30 years. I haven't had a single person fail yet. You can get yourself some wetsuits in the hut back there if you want to grab one of those and then I've got some forms for you to sign.'

Ellie had sensed my nervousness and was loving it.

'What's the form for, Jerry? Is that in case we get eaten by sharks?'

'Ellie! You're not helping. You know I don't like open water.'

And I didn't. I don't know if this was linked to being terrified of Jaws or maybe even struggling to put my feet flat on the floor in the deep end of the local swimming baths during school swimming galas, as my stomach turned at the smell of chlorine in the air, coupled with a look of panic as James Chow's verruca sock and Darren Bower's bobbing vomit had their own race along one of the swimming lanes.

I waddled out of the wake boarding shed in my wetsuit. They only had brown left in my size.

I looked at Ellie, who obviously looked stunning in hers. She eyed me up and down, smiled and did a faux tiger's roar.

'Grreeeoww... You look good Danny. Shows off those legs of yours. You look like a sexy, rubbery buffalo.'

I'd never been called that before.

'Ellie. How do you manage to look like a James Bond girl on every single date we have? Look at me. I look like a massive traumatised seal. As soon as I fall off that surfboard thing, I'm done for. I'll get

eaten alive.'

Ellie started to hum the Jaws music as we made our way back to Jerry, who was doing some very energetic limbering up at the edge of the water.

I nudged Ellie.

'Do you think he still uses the word rad to describe things?'

'He definitely does. You ok Danny? Are you a bit more relaxed now? You do look good in that wetsuit you know? I don't think I've ever fancied you more.'

Ellie gave me a quick kiss before speeding up and walking towards the edge of the water. It could be worse; I thought to myself. She could have picked xylophone lessons.

'Woohooooo that was AMAZING! Let's go again!!'

Ellie was a natural. Jerry was singing her praises and immediately answered one of our questions.

'That spin you did was RAD, Ellie. You should have tried it Danny... you were doing pretty good yourself.'

'Yeah, I was kind of half rad, I think. I felt a bit seasick when we first went out if I'm honest.'

'Danny... what's our Y date going to be? I guess it's not going to be yachting?'

'It's definitely not going to be yachting, no....I haven't decided yet...come on let's get all of this wet gear off. Hang gliding next...'

I was apprehensive. Human kites were definitely not my thing. But bravado was setting in.

'Pretty windy up here isn't it, Danny?'

'WHAT??'

'Oh.Yeah.We'll be alright though.Wind is good for hang gliding probably. I think. I can't wait to get out there. Free as a bird and all that.'

'Danny.'

'Yeah?'

'I don't think I want to do it.'

I'd never been more relieved in my life. And whereas previously I would have maintained the bravado for a few more minutes, that was no longer the way. No more games. No more fanfare. No more needless drama. Just give her reassurance.

'We won't do it.'

'You sure? Look at Phil over there. He's got his goggles on. And a helmet. Are you sure we don't have to do it?'

'He looks like he's struggling with the goggles, the helmet and also that big human kite thing he's trying to lift up as well.We won't do it.'

That night, Ellie seemed down again.

'I didn't complete the walk in Spain and now I said no to the hang gliding. I'm rubbish at this.'

'Look at me.You're not rubbish.You're amazing. And you're beautiful. Hey, we did the wake boarding didn't we. And I'll let you into a secret.'

'What secret?'

'I didn't really want to go hang gliding either. If you wouldn't have said no then I would have. Did you see the fella in charge?

He was about seventy years old. And he had a pen behind his ear. How is someone with a pen behind his ear going to save us if we get into trouble in mid-air? Superman never had a pen behind his ear. He didn't say to Lois Lane just before he took her soaring through Metropolis 'Lois, just before we set off, can you pass me that biro please?'

'I know you're just trying to make me feel better Danny but I feel like I've failed again.'

'Ok, I know what to do. I think I've got our letter Y date.'

'Because of today?'

'Because of today. We were both going to say no to this hang-gliding experience, right?'

'Yeah.'

'So, let's do a day of saying Yes to things. We'll have a Yes Day.'

I knew she liked the idea straight away.

Someone putting their arms around you and nestling their head into your chest is always a good sign.

Yes Day

I hadn't seen Tom for a few weeks and the catch up was happening in his local coffee shop.

'Burton Coggles Country Fayre? You're taking Ellie on a date to Burton Coggles Country Fayre? She took you to fucking Venice, Danny. You've said you want to marry this girl and you're taking her to Burton Coggles Country Fayre?'

'Stop saying Burton Coggles Country Fayre.'

'BUT YOU'RE TAKING HER TO BURTON COGGLES COUNTRY FAYRE. This is the Y date, right? And not the 'why?' date as in 'WHY ARE YOU TAKING SOMEONE TO BURTON COGGLES COUNTRY FUCKING FAYRE.'

'It'll be good! There'll be animals to pet…raffles…Ellie loves all of that and so do I.'

'Right ok fair enough. Let's have a recap. You did an X-Treme sports date and you're still here to tell the tale.'

'There's one good reason for that, Tom.'

'Go on.'

'You weren't there.'

'Look, that Scafell Pike thing wasn't my fault. It was the weather's fault. Plus, you offered me a cheese sandwich. You know cheese makes me go blind. Anyway, alpha male…what's the Y Date? Because I know it's the penultimate letter in the alphabet. I know my alphabet very well and Burton Coggles Country Fayre does NOT begin with the letter Y.'

'We're going to have a day of yes.'

'Wait a minute. A day of yes? You're not going to...you know...are you?'

'Going to you know...what?'

'You know...you're not going to ask one of the MOST important questions a person can ask?'

'You mean 'Why did Anthony Worrall Thompson rob a mountain of cheese when he must have had easy access to dairy products?'

'No... not that important question, although it is a very important and legitimate question. You know. THE important question. It's a yes day. Are you...are you going to ask her to marry you?'

'Well. You know that Tarot reading we went to? When we went in separate rooms? We both pulled the Page of Pentacles card.'

'NOT THE PAGE OF PENTACLES CARD!! What's the page of pentacles card?'

'It's about seizing love. And Ellie picked the major cards for Love and Justice as well. Something about signing contracts...so that could suggest...you know. Marriage?'

'It could suggest anything. How many cards are in a Tarot deck, Danny?'

'No idea. Hang on let me look on my phone. It iiiis...78 cards.'

'And how many did you both pick at your six-month readings?'

'Erm...three main ones and then six more...one for each month.'

'Ok...so...the odds of you picking the same card are about. one in nine. If you want to base your life on something that happens one out of every nine times by chance. that's entirely up to you. What else did you both get told?'

'There'll be a trip over water. You'll pass water at some point soon.'

'You'll both pass water at some point soon? Danny, every single person on earth has a piss at least once a day. It's nonsense. I've told you…the odds of you both picking the same card out is roughly a one in nine chance.'

'Alright, Charlie Babbit. You know maths has never really been my thirte.'

'What?'

'Sorry, forte. Maths has never really been my forte. Look I know these tarot readers aren't fortune tellers. It's all more to do with suggestion…but sometimes I just need that little push or confirmation. Anyway, it's more than that, Tom. I just know.'

'Ok look. I know you do. And I'm happy for you. And I know I can be cynical but I just worry about you sometimes. Like mates do. I'll get us another coffee.'

'Can I have another expresso please?'

'Danny. It's espresso. You're doing that on purpose. You know it winds me up.'

'I know, Tom. Like mates do.'

As I expected, Burton Coggles Country Fayre excited Ellie a lot more than it did Tom.

'I can't WAIT for today, Danny! A day of YES!'

'Saying yes to things can change your life, Ellie. Someone said it on a bus to someone many years ago and that person's life changed completely. He even ended up getting married.'

The look at each other again. There's something in the air. Does she think today might be the day? Surely a restaurant in Venice would be more of a proposal venue than The

152

Burton Coggles Country Fayre. Plus, I've already seen a stall selling pulled pork sandwiches with a 5-star hygiene rating sticker plastered on it and there are four clumps of dog muck on the grass next to it. There's no way I would propose at The Burton Coggles Country Fayre.

'Let's go and get a coffee and a milky tea.'

'Yes!'

'Good start, Ellie…you're getting the hang of it already.'

'Yes!'

'Ok, that's enough. Settle down. Here… I'll get these. Hi, can we have a black coffee and a milky tea please.'

'Do you want milk in the black coffee?'

'Sorry?'

'Do you want milk in the black coffee?'

Now I know Burton Coggles is a little bit in the middle of fucking nowhere and a lot of the locals seem a little bit vacant but surely one of the main components of a black coffee is no milk.

But rules are rules. For today at least. I sighed as Ellie laughed. *'Yes…please.'*

'Ok, so that's a milky tea and a black coffee with milk…and would you like a slice of cake or a cookie to go with that?'

'No than…oh actually, yes. Yes, we'll have a slice of cake and a cookie as well please.'

Ellie smiled at me knowing we'd completed our first official yeses of the day. We sat down and clinked our mugs.

'Cheers Ellie. Here's to yes day.'

'Cheers! Can you pass me one of those forks…let's get stuck into this lemon drizzle cake.' And before I could tell my Snoop Dogg lemon shizzle cake and Wu Tang Flan jokes, I managed to clumsily throw and drop the fork onto the floor, towards Ellie's feet.

'Here, I'll get it', I said, bending down on one knee and looking up at her.

As I knelt in front of her, our eyes locked. That look again. Just between us and as if no one else in the world existed.

A shiver ran down my spine as she half smiled.

We both knew it was never going to happen here. Not in the Burton Coggles Country Fayre. But something was definitely in the air.

'I thought you'd put an engagement ring in the lemon drizzle cake for a minute there.'

'Yeah…how funny would that have been…I tell you what, Ellie…I'm going to propose…'

'What?'

'No! Er…I'm going to propose we go outside and find some more things to say yes to. Come on, let's go.'

We headed outside in to the fields, which were littered with colourful stalls and country folk wandering around.

'I love these days with you, Danny. Just the two of us. Wandering around. Holding hands. Picking things off each other's faces. Having fun. It's all I need. Come on, let's go this way.'

'Hello, you two…you both look very arty and creative. Especially you, madam. I LOVE your ear-rings…how would you like a

temporary tattoo for today? Only five pounds.'

'Do we want to get temporary tattoos, Ellie? I think we know the answer to that.'

Ellie nodded, as she fiddled with her ear-rings. For someone who received so many compliments, I loved her awkwardness and vulnerability when a stranger would pay her one.

Half an hour later, me and Ellie were sporting matching burnt orange butterfly tattoos on our forearms.

'Hey, look at yours, Danny. Did you ask for that little moustache on it? Mine's a little bit smaller than yours. I love it though. I might get a permanent one.'

Ellie was admiring her new artwork in between giggling at the impressive marrow that had just been voted 'most impressive marrow' at yet another random stall.

We were approached by a lady looking quite flustered and as far as I could tell, I don't think she'd even laid eyes upon the impressive marrow yet.

'Hey! I don't know if you can help or if you're interested but we need two more judges for the prettiest pig competition...it starts in five minutes. One of the judges has been drinking Scrumpy since 9 o'clock this morning. He was shouting that his wee was starting to smell of apples and to be totally honest, he was beginning to scare the pigs. His wife had to take him home and she was judging too.'

Me and Ellie looked at each other and shouted in unison.

'YES!!'

We were led through a field and were met by six pink, muddy competitors, none of whom were very pretty at all.

'Pssss-wsss Pssss-wssss.'

'Why are you psss-wsssing them, Ellie? They're not cats'

'I know but animals normally react to psss-wsss. How is a pig not to know pssss-wssss? I'm voting for the one that reacts to psssss-wsssss. Awwwww look at him. I want that one. It looks like he's wearing high heels. And look at his pink eyelashes. Let's vote for him. Psss- wsss.'

Ellie always seemed excited when she was with animals. Or so I thought.

Everything was about to change in a heartbeat. Everything.

'Horse riding this way, you two! You look as if you could both handle a horse. Come on, cowboy...and cowgirl.'

Another Yes opportunity if ever there was one.

'Yes! Come on Ellie, let's go. Hey, we can have a race.'

I reached out to grab her hand but she was frozen stiff. She was looking down at her feet.

'I can't do it, Danny. No.'

'What? What do you mean you can't do it? Come on, it's Yes day!'

'Danny. No. Please don't make me do it.'

'Ellie? What is it?'

And right there and then, she broke down. A flood of tears.

And I witnessed the kind of sob I had only heard twice previously when a similar noise had escaped my own grief-stricken body.

'Ellie, it's ok. We won't do it. We don't have to do anything you don't want to do.'

She was quivering.

The sob was the kind of crying with an inward breath and no noise, until her body finally allowed her to speak, slowly and quietly.

'She was too young, Danny. She was so small. And she loved horses so much. Mum and dad trusted me to take her to the stables. And now I can't bring her back.'

Another long inward breath and no noise.

Fuck. What is she telling me? How do I react? Is she telling me what I think she's telling me?

'Ellie. Give me your hand. Come with me...come and sit over here.'

I reached for Ellie's hand and led her over to a bench, as far away and out of sight of the two horses who were lazily nodding their heads back and forth, nonchalantly grazing upon grass, unaware of the person sat next to me, shaking and trying her best to squeeze my hand.

'What happened Ellie? Tell me. Come on, it's ok. It's me. I'm here. You can tell me.'

Through sobs and whimpers, interspersed with the long inward breaths with no noise, Ellie began to speak.

'We took her to A and E and sat and waited for hours. It felt like days. Mum and Dad were telling me it was alright and everything was going to be ok but I was so scared, Danny. Dad had his arm around me. He was protecting me, I remember. I wanted someone to wake me up and tell me it was a nightmare and everything was normal and she was in our bedroom with me and I was reading her a story and putting her hair in a pony tail. She loved it when I'd read her a story and put her hair in a pony tail. The doctor walked in. You shouldn't know what that face means at thirteen years old

but I remember looking at him when he walked through the door. He didn't need to speak. I still see his face. I still see it. Most days. And I see my Mum's face screaming. Her whole face looked like it was screaming. I only see it. I don't hear it. I don't hear the wails. Because there was no sound. Not in my mind. Not in my memory. But I know there must have been sound, Danny. There must have been because her mouth was wide open. And her eyes are screaming, too. And Dad's hugging her and I'm just watching them. Then I'm looking at the doctor again. He still hasn't spoken to us, Danny. Mum's mouth is still open. But I can't hear anything. But I know there's sound. Then I just see my black shoes. I'm just staring at my black shoes. I'm looking down staring at my black shoes. I'm looking down. I'm looking down. And then I'm home.'

What do I say? My heart feels ripped out as she empties hers to me. All I can say is how I feel.

'Ellie. I'm here.'

I wanted her to know there was no need to be afraid. But how?

'I'll miss her forever, Danny. I'll miss her every day of my life and I know I'll meet her again someday. She's the star that still guides me and I miss her so, so much.'

Ellie smiled slightly in between tears. Fucking hell. Even when she's crying, she's beautiful.

'Hey. Look up. Look at me. You were here for me when I told you about my Mum and Dad. I'm here for you now. Listen. You're not alone. I'm here for you. You're not alone.'

'I don't know where she is, Danny. But I'll find her one day and we'll be together again. Sometimes I'll hear her name in my sleep and I'll wake up and I'll cry. I feel so helpless most of the time. I get down. I look down. I always look down. I just feel so...black and

white. *So black and white. I just always feel so black and white.'*

Now I know what to say. For once in my life, I know exactly what to say.

'Ellie. Look at me.You're not black and white. Look at me.You're the colour. And I'm here for you and you can talk to me. I'll try and help you. I will help you. Every single person who meets you, loves you straight away.You've got a gift.You change people. For the better.You've changed me. For the better. And you've got to keep giving your gift and never change how you are because everyone loves you. I love you. So fucking much.You're not black and white. You're the colour, Ellie...you might not see it but everyone else does.'

Ellie looked at me and her face began to contort even more. The inward breath and no noise.

So, I told her again. *'You're the colour, Ellie.You're the colour.'*

And as she fell into my arms, I held her tighter than I'd ever held her before.

Gemma Hindle

I'm 37 years old. I've come up with an idea to try and finally meet 'The One.' An A-to-Z dating game. Me and Gemma Hindle did quite well. We reached the letter I. Ice Skating. Nine dates. Gemma Hindle wasn't the one. But I'm going to continue searching.

Maybe I'll meet her one day.

Zain

'She said she feels black and white, Tom.'

It killed me every time I thought about it. About what had happened to her all those years ago. To her little sister. And how Ellie had perceived herself ever since.

I was the one who felt black and white.

The same black and white as I'd felt before I met Tom as a shy sixteen-year-old, before he became the first person to properly bring colour into my life.

'Listen to this band, Danny.'

'Come and meet my friends this weekend with me, Danny.'

'We haven't got a lift? Who cares. Let's hitchhike instead, Danny.'

We'd had times in our lives when we hadn't seen each other for years. But would always gravitate back to each other.

As good friends do.

'I can't believe that's how she feels, Danny. Every single person who meets her loves her straight away. She's got a gift. She changes people. I've seen it with my own eyes.'

'I just wish she could see it, Tom. And I'm going to make her see it. Trust me.'

'I think I've got something that could help.'

'What do you mean?'

'Ok. And I can't believe I'm even doing this but…you know you

said Ellie's choice for Z was this Zain character, another tarot night? I've printed this for you to give to Ellie beforehand.'

Tom handed me an envelope. I opened it and unfolded the paper inside.

'A birth chart? For Ellie? But you think it's all hocus pocus. You're the biggest sceptic I know.'

'You're right. I don't believe in it. At all. But I know how to help my friends. And friends of my friends.'

'Fuck. Thank you. That's really...decent of you.'

'I'm decent, Danny. I'm really decent. But that's me, isn't it? Typical Taurus.'

Tom walked over to the bar for our final two pints and final two packets of salted peanuts before my alphabet dating game was to come to an end. He gave me a squeeze on the shoulder on the way past, which sometimes, between friends, can mean more than a thousand words.

The following morning my phone peeped. It was Ellie's peep.

'Hey. You all set for Zain's tomorrow? 7pm? x'

'Can't wait. Did you get the letter? It should have arrived this morning?'

'What letter? Hang on, I've just parked up. Give me a min x'

Earlier that morning, I'd called at Ellie's and posted her birth chart with an accompanying hand written letter.

'Hi Ellie. It's me. Danny. The Sagittarius. Going a bit old school with a letter here...but seeing as we're doing our 26th and final letter soon, I thought one more letter wouldn't hurt. It's your birth chart. Have you opened it yet? I bet you have. I bet you opened *that bit first didn't you. It's got all those little symbols that I don't understand on it. The squiggly lion one. The moon on a skateboard one. And the devil wearing deely boppers one. I've highlighted my favourite parts. The parts I see in you. And why I love you. The orange highlighter was running out. Sorry about that. I'm rambling. You look very pretty by the way.*

I'd highlighted 8 parts of the birth chart in 8 different, bright colours.

You have a sense of individuality and outward-shining creative energy.

You love to start anything new and can accomplish anything you desire.

You are bold, but even when you are quiet you are brave in your own way.

You're a unique, independent personality.

You are a self-motivated with a forceful personality and a strong will.

You are popular, are attractive to people and your self-confidence and security make you easy to deal with on many levels.

You are very witty; others enjoy your playful and sometimes mischievous sense of humour.

You have optimism and always want to do the right thing and say the right things to people.

I could go on and on with these myself, Ellie and make my own up. But I've tried to do it officially from your birth chart. It's how I see you. I could have used hundreds of examples of my own with a hundred different colours but I've just used those 8 colours above. Well 7 and the dry orange one. It's how I see you. How I will always see you. And how more than anything I want you to see yourself.

You're the colour.

Danny x

Around an hour later, my phone peeped again. It was Ellie's peep.

'I'm crying x'

'You ok?'

'I've just read your letter and the birth chart. Thank you. I'm going to try. I'm really going to try, starting from now. Starting tonight. I'll see you at Zain's at 7pm. You've got the address. I'll pick you up some orange highlighters x'

The 26th and final date was Ellie's choice.

A tarot reader named Zain.

A three-card reading and this time we were sitting in together for a joint reading. Ellie had asked me to get there first and said that she'd see me there.

Maybe she's done me a birth chart? Do I want a birth chart? Do I need a birth chart? I know how I feel about her. I can't let the turn of a tarot card change that?

Can I?

I'm not going to let a virtual stranger shape the destiny of my future.

Our future.

Ellie's the one. I'm convinced of it. I love her. I have to do the right thing. 6:50pm.

I knock on the front door.

A gentleman wearing glasses, a purple jumper and jeans with possibly too many patches on, opens the door.

'BARRY!!!'

'Hello. Erm, no, it's Danny. Are you…Zain?'

'Danny!!! Sorry. I don't know who Barry is. I think it's all this incense in the house. Plays havoc with my brain cells, I'm sure the damn stuff is rotting them away. Anyway, come in! Come on through! I'll take you through to Zain.'

I was led down the hallway, through a door and into a long living room. It was dark but flickering lights lit up various buddha statues and certificates on shelves, adorning dozens of tarot and astrology books.

A dark figure was sat in the corner and emerged from within the shadows as meditative music floated through the room.

'Hi Sagittarius.'

I squinted, barely making out a face I was certain I recognised from somewhere.

'I've been waiting to see you for a while, Danny. Have you had any more of those meatballs recently?'

'Zain?'

The lady I had first met in Amalia restaurant and then at the Health and Wellbeing Day before crossing paths yet again at the restaurant was stood two feet away from me.

'That's me. Zain. Come on. Come over and take a seat. Black coffee, right?'

'Yeah…black coffee would be great, thanks…'

'Barry, can you get Danny a black coffee please. And I'll have a tea. And can you remember the sugar this time?'

'Your husband's name is Barry?'

'It is. He's harmless isn't he. A bit forgetful sometimes…why do you ask?'

'Oh nothing, it's just that when he opened the door, he shouted BARRY! I… erm…it doesn't matter, I'm rambling. I'm getting butterflies already. I don't know why it happens but every time I see a tarot reader, I get butterflies. Are we going to start already, I thought it was a joint reading? Shouldn't we wait until Ellie…'

Zain interrupted.

'There we go, just sit right here. We can get prepared. I just need you to close your eyes, uncross your arms and breathe three times. Deeply.

In for the count of four.

Out for the count of four.

In for the count of four.

Out for the count of four.

In for the count of four.

Out for the count of four.

A knock on the living room door.

I opened my eyes. I felt calmer. The nerves and butterflies were beginning to subside.

And Ellie slowly peered around the door and walked in towards the empty chair placed next to mine. She was wearing small round glasses. A baggy jumper. Flared jeans. Tiny white trainers. She looked beautiful.

'Hiya Zain.'

'Hi Ellie.'

Wait.

'You two know each other?'

I looked at Ellie. The smile. The fucking smile.

'I've been seeing Zain for years, Danny. Ever since I was old enough to come and see her. I wanted guidance. Needed guidance. After what happened. Anything to help me get over it. I needed help. Zain said I'd meet someone. Someone kind. Someone who'd help me.'

I sat upright in my chair. Arms still unfolded. Still breathing deeply.

In for the count of four. Out for the count of four.

In for the count of four. Out for the count of four.

In for the count of four. Out for the count of four.

And Ellie held my hand.

And then it happened again.

The exact same feeling from La Meseta in Santiago.

A kind of energy and release which I can only describe as being like a thousand shivers down my spine leaving my body as I sat.

I felt like crying but I couldn't.

I felt like screaming but I couldn't.

I felt like swallowing. But I couldn't.

Ellie held my hand even tighter and my mind flashed back like an animated pocket flick book, opening up and uncovering a canon of memories.

I see Ellie walking in to Amalia with her arms outstretched. Hi Ellie. The hug. I see Zain in the background. There she is. I see her. A bookstore. A cinema date. A double date…An evening stroll. My dad. I SEE my dad. Hi dad. Ellie's here now. He's waving at me. I see a solitary burnt orange butterfly fly away. I see the fairground, we're stuck on a ghost train, I see a Scrabble board and a friend moonwalking, I'm reading a leaflet. I see you again, Zain. You're there. I can see you. I see Ellie holding my hand. We're ice skating. We're watching jazz. We're singing karaoke. We're at the lake. We're in each other's arms. I love you, Ellie. A movie night. A night in. My mum. I SEE my mum. Hi mum. Ellie's here now. She's waving at me. I see a solitary burnt orange butterfly fly away. A night out. I see Ellie. In a taxi. She's got her head down. She's looking down. No. Please look up. Please come back. Please. Come. Back. We're reading poems. We're at a quiz. We're in Amalia again. I see Zain. There she is. We're in Spain. I see two burnt orange butterflies and I'm dropped to my knees. They're gone. The butterflies have gone. I see Simon reading my tarot cards. He smiles at me. Ellie is next door. She's with Zain. I see her. We're watching a film. We have sweets. Venice. Wine tasting. Xtreme sports. I see a day of Yes. I see Ellie. She's young. I see a small coffin. Brilliant white. Flowers. So many flowers. I see Ellie looking down at her shoes. She looks so smart. But she's looking down. She's crying. She's looking down. And I see a solitary burnt orange butterfly above her. She's safe now.

'Danny!! Helloooo!! Are you therrre??'

Ellie's voice snapped me suddenly back into the room.

And the feeling of a thousand shivers down my spine stopped just as suddenly as it had started.

Zain was sat opposite me. She was looking at me as if she'd seen what I'd seen. As if she knew.

As if she'd always known.

167

Barry stumbled into the living room, just about managing not to spill a tray full of cups and plates over us.

'There we go. A coffee for the gentleman. Tea with sugar for my lovely Zain and the usual for you, Ellie. Milky tea.'

Ellie continued to hold my hand and squoze it even tighter. She rubbed my thumb with hers and looked at me with the deep, deep, green manga eyes.

And we both breathed deeply

In for the count of four.

Out for the count of four.

In for the count of four.

Out for the count of four.

In for the count of four.

Out for the count of four.

And very slowly and very deliberately, Zain proceeded to turn three cards upwards and onto the table.

Acknowledgements.

Hello. You look very nice today.

Every story ever told began with a yes.

'Why don't you go and see a tarot reader, Paul?'

And I'm not sceptical. I'm very open minded. So, I said yes.

And the tarot reader told me I had an idea. But that the idea was locked. And I needed to unlock it.

So, she gave me a stone which looked like a white feather.

One week later, while out running, the idea suddenly dropped. 'What if someone who *didn't* believe in astrology, horoscopes and tarot reading met someone who *was* into astrology, horoscopes and tarot reading. And what if they had 26 dates. One date for every letter of the alphabet.

And as I continued running, the title dropped. 'Alpha Male'. And then I got so excited, I forgot I was running across a main road and I nearly got hit by a car.

And six months later I'd finished writing Alpha Male.

But not without the help, advice and guidance of some very clever, generous, funny people. Nice people. People who open doors for people.

Paula and Lisa, who, once I knew were massively into horoscopes and tarot reading, were my go-to people, putting up with me as I'd bore them with incessant questions. What about this? Why this? How about this? Would a Sagittarian say this? Thank you for all your support, advice and for the birth charts.

Issie (Issie Green) for offering valuable insight into the

characters and the ideas.

Gill...for being Ellie in our read through. For your genuine comedy insight and advice about everything. And for being funny. I like that in people.

Warren...for your impressions and your advice on jokes. And for being funny. I like that in people.

Ian. For saying 'Let's book the flights then' and starting a journey, walking in Spain, which I hope leads to more and more walks in Spain and around the world. It's the best experience I've had and I wouldn't want to do it with anyone else. And I'd never have written this book without those experiences. Caminamos juntos.

And lastly, Colin. I genuinely could not have written this without you. Because you gave me this keyboard in 2015, remember?

No. Serious face. Come on, Paul. You can do this.

Col, I can't thank you enough. And not just for the legal stuff, which I had no idea about. I mean the genuine stuff. For being a friend. For offering advice on where Danny and Ellie would go on a date. For the random phone calls. 'What about if they did this?' 'How about if you did that?' and for one of the most important things anyone has ever said to me, when I was getting over excited about this whole idea.

'Paul. See that fella at the end of the bar? He doesn't give a fuck about your book. Just relax.'

Everyone needs a friend like that. And I'm proud to call you mine.

Ytterbia though?

And to that fella at the end of the bar. I hope you do read this book. I hope lots of people read it. Maybe you'll start your own Alphabet Dating with your loved one? You should do. But do it with someone nice.

Nice people attract nice people.

Thanks for reading.

Paul x